I0628447

Before the Sun

~ An Inspirational Fiction Novel

The Prequel to the Psalms 37 Novel Series

Shakira R. Thompson

BELIEVER'S CHOICE
MEDIA

Before The Sun

Before The Sun

Printed in the United States of America

Titles are available at special discounts for bulk purchases by corporations, institutions, and other organizations.

Believer's Choice Media

P.O. Box 2131
Yulee, FL 32041
www.shakirabelieves.com

Before The Sun
Cover Designed by: Gad Savage

Library of Congress Congress Control Number: TBD

ISBN: 978-0-9906725-9-3 (p)

Scripture quotations are taken from the *Holy Bible*, King James, NIV, and Common English Bible Versions.

Before The Sun is a work of fiction. All characters and places appearing in this work are fictitious. Any resemblance to real persons, living or dead, places, establishments, events, organizations, and/or locations is purely coincidental and a product of the author's mind.

First Printing, 2016

To my team, what we're creating is nothing short of a miracle.

———————————

ACKNOWLEDGEMENTS

Here we are again, another year and another book...God is so good. Who knew there was a story to be told prior to the inaugural Psalms 37 series, I certainly didn't when I first wrote *High Noon Justice* but that goes to show you what I know. ☺

Since the last book, *Unforsaken*, in this past year, I have gone through and experienced A LOT.

Through physical deaths and spiritual ones, I've lost friends but also through grace, I've made new ones. As such, I've learned a great deal about the circle of life.

This year has provided me with so many opportunities to learn and grow and while some of the lessons were tough to learn, I'm grateful for the good, the bad, the ugly, and even the real ugly.

My first acknowledgement will always be to Father God, my heavenly Father, He knows more about me than I do myself and shows me on a daily basis how He's with me, even when I can't see Him. Father God, I'm grateful.

There wouldn't be one word written without the love and support given and shown to me from the Thompson crew, my husband, Keith M. Thompson and our two beautiful daughters. Thank you to my oldest for your gentle pushes of encouragement, you inspire me to always finish. I appreciate the love and support of my youngest whose smile and rubs across my shoulders let me know that I can do anything.

To Gad Savage, we just keep getting better with time. I appreciate your willingness to work with me until I say, "I love it." Thank you for all of the graphic designs you do for me, I don't take your kindness for granted.

I can never forget to thank the beta readers who take out time from their busy schedules to read what's been between the pages, sometimes the craziness I feel that comes out of my head but they read it and help me become better and better. To Gene and Genine Adams, Samarra St. Hilaire, LaQuieta Huey, Dee Jackson, Poarche' Clark, and Deborah Dunson, I appreciate you and love you ladies to life.

To the Shakira's Sweethearts, the baddest book club this side of heaven, your support, love, and kindness shown towards me is never lost and taken for granted. I appreciate each of you.

To my parents, I need you to know without you, I wouldn't be here to acknowledge anyone.

Because of the blessings you've spoken over me and provided me with, I, in turn, bless and honor you.

It is important for you to know as I publicly affirm you two of your Godly characteristics you both exhibit that you are the blessed parents of myself and my sister. You are the blessed grandparents of the fabulous five. Growing in grace, may you continue to yield fruit and flourish. Thank you for your prayers and unwavering support, I hope you know how much I truly love you, thank you.

If you are holding this book in your hands and reading these words, then I also acknowledge and thank you as well, I'm grateful you'd take the time to read words I've written. It truly means a lot to me.

My grandmother Eliza, always said to us, "People don't have to do anything for you." Boy, do I miss her and boy wasn't she right? She shaped a lot of my core beliefs and values and that is one I hold near and dear. People don't have to do anything for you and so as a result of all you do, I say from the bottom of my heart, **THANK YOU!**

Prologue

"Man, I can't believe you. Kevin, we just got out of church and you are already calling me about going out tonight...not going to happen, captain."

Displaying a wide grin and dressed with finesse in a custom designed suit, Carson Montgomery stood talking and laughing on his cellphone.

Kevin Lofton, childhood friend of Carson asked, "Where are you now? Are you at Sunday dinner or are you still at the church?"

"Yeah, I'm still at the church, I'm probably going to skip dinner, why do you ask?" Carson replied.

With firm intentions in his voice, Kevin explained, "C'mon, Carson man, this is the last week before you get hitched man, you have to come out with us. We hitting up all the spots and you know how we do, player. Not only that, the fellas and I are planning a real special treat, just for you and it starts tonight, we have something planned every night. I'm trying to be on my best man duties and you are tripping."

Needing to sit down and reflect, Carson found the nearest pew, rubbing the middle of his forehead and checking his watch for the time.

In his mind, Carson sat pondering the pros and cons of the temptation from Kevin's proposal as opposed to the proposal, he'd already made.

Blowing a massive amount of air out through his cheeks, Carson replied, "Hey man, I appreciate the effort but you know my lady and her family arrives this evening and their welcome reception is tonight. Trust me, there is no way I could go out with you guys even if I wanted to."

Asking a pointed question, Kevin inquired, "So what you're really saying is, you want to go and I need to create a way for you to be able to go, right, right? You know I got you man, that's what we do, who do I need to call, who do I need to talk to? You want me to call Bishop?"

Looking down at his phone, Carson replied laughing, "Kev, man...you're crazy. No, I don't want you to call Bishop. In fact, did you hear anything he said in service today?"

Mocking Bishop Montgomery's voice, Kevin said, "And the Lord said...yeah, yeah, yeah, I heard him. So, you trying to slide tonight or not?"

Smiling and slowly shaking his head, Carson answered, "What am I going to do with you man? Your impersonation of Bishop is whack. My daddy don't sound nothing like that. But hey, listen and please listen to me this time, I will not be going out with you guys tonight. No strip clubs for me...tonight."

"Oh, so I get it, you're going to get little miss pretty in town this evening, get her all settled and then we're going out tomorrow night, right, right?" Kevin asked laughing.

"Wrong, wrong...," Carson exclaimed as he noticed his father, Bishop Montgomery entering the sanctuary. "Hey look, I'm going to catch up with you guys later on, alright. Peace."

"Uh Carson, did I hear someone say something about a strip club in the house of the Lord?" Bishop asked.

Nervously laughing, Carson said, "Oh no Bishop, you might want to get your ears checked. What you heard was me talking to Kevin about the grip on his club. You know, the golf outing, the Wedding Week Invitational...just one of the many activities the church has planned for us."

"Oh, maybe I do need to get my ears checked, but that's great, I'm glad Kevin is getting his clubs together." Thrusting his chest with a hearty laugh and placing his hand on Carson's shoulder, "Ah yes, your mother and I are looking forward to wedding week, we are so excited. The church's event planners have all sorts of things planned. They've planned banquets, parties, shows, concerts, you name it. Boy, I tell you, what an exciting time, huh?" Bishop exclaimed.

Wringing his hands in an attempt to squeeze in some excitement, Carson answered, "Oh, uh, yeah Bishop...exciting times indeed; I can't wait."

Clapping his hands in sheer delight, Bishop shouted, "That's my boy; I'm so glad to hear it. My first born, my namesake is getting ready to take on a wife and get married. You know son, you've made a fine choice in Scarlett; I'm so proud of you son."

Lowering his head, Carson simply said, "Thanks Bishop."

With a hand over his heart, Bishop looked up saying, "Oh, the power of choice." Shaking his head and in a softer tone, Bishop continued, "You've made a wonderful choice son."

Tilting his head towards his father, Carson asked, "Bishop, are you alright?"

Solemnly speaking, Bishop countered, "Yes, yes son; I just believe she's the one, she's the one we've been praying for and I thank God for her, especially after your last -."

Interrupting his father, Carson shrieked and said, "Uh Bishop, um remember you said, we weren't to ever, like ever discuss that again? So yeah, let's not talk about that, let's just forget it ever happened.

Breathing a heavy sigh, Bishop Montgomery, looked at Carson saying, "Exactly. To God be the Glory we were able to contain that. Now you see why I'm constantly thanking God for Scarlett. You need someone to tame you down, boy. Someone who will straighten you out so you can take over the church one day. I'm not planning to pastor this great church all of my life like my daddy did. You, my boy, are the future of this wonderful ministry so I hope you finally have yourself together and are ready to do right by Scarlett."

A glimmer of light showed up behind Carson's hazel-colored eyes, "Yes sir, the church. Yes, I'm ready, this church is in my blood, it's in my DNA, it's my birthright. Bishop, you are so right, Scarlett is exactly what I need in order to take over the reigns of the church."

"Two of my most favorite men." Regina Montgomery said entering the sanctuary.

"Hello Mother." Carson grinned greeting First Lady Regina.

"Hey there sweetheart." Bishop said smiling at his wife as he kissed her hand.

Turning towards Carson, Regina offered, "Carson, everything is all prepared and set up for the reception later. What time will Scarlett and her family be arriving?"

Checking his watch again, Carson answered his mother, "I'll be leaving here soon, their flight lands in about two hours. I'll pick them up and bring them back here like you told me to do, Mother."

Squealing and fluttering around, Regina said, "I know, I know...I'm just so excited." Kissing Carson on the cheek, Regina said, "My baby boy is getting married and Carson, you couldn't be marrying a more beautiful person than Scarlett. I just love her so and I know she's going to make a wonderful first lady."

Inching closer and closer to Regina, Bishop snuggled next to his wife and said, "Yeah son, the bible says, he who finds a wife, finds a good thing and obtains favor from the Lord. We are so glad you found your good thing. Lord knows how happy I am that I found mine."

Offering light sarcasm and in a dismissive tone, Regina countered, "C'mon now Eugene, you know good and well you didn't find me, your parents did."

Clasping his hands under his chin in a prayer gesture, Bishop said, "Nah, they just led me to you, the woman I'd prayed for. It's all in how you look at it my dearest Regina."

Sharing in a family laugh, Carson feeling uncomfortable between his parent's romance, changed the subject, "You know it's a real shame my own brothers won't be here for my wedding."

Trading Bishop's hand for Carson's, Regina looked at Carson saying, "I know son but the mission trip they're on is very important and couldn't be changed. You said you understood. Carson, you do realize as you begin to take over this ministry, there will be times where you have to make important decisions like this. Everyone can't be in two places at once."

"She's right you know." Bishop echoed.

Laughing longer than usual, Carson shifted in his seat as he was distracted by Michelle Oliver walking towards him and his parents.

"Hello Bishop and First Lady; I was sent in here to tell you that you're needed in the reception area." Michelle announced.

Scratching his head, Bishop asked, "They need both of us?"

Trying to sound convincing, "Yeah, I guess it has something to do about tonight's reception." Michelle explained as she, on the sly rubbed her hand across Carson's shoulder blade.

Noticing the gesture, Regina clears her throat, "Carson darling, I think you should probably get going as well, you don't want to be late picking up your bride, right?"

"Yes mother, you're right; I'll leave right now." Carson replied.

Leaning in to kiss on the cheek and serving squinted eyes at Michelle, Regina proudly proclaimed, "That's my boy...go and get our girl."

Chapter 1

Rushing to get closer to Carson, "Thank goodness; I thought they'd never leave. I've been waiting to see you all day. Now, I'm happy that we're finally all alone."

Pushing Michelle away, "Stop it; we're in the church for crying out loud. Get a hold of yourself Michelle. We can't do this; we won't do this."

Unwilling to concede, Michelle walked back closer to Carson, wrapping her arms around his waist and said softly, "That's not what you said last night."

"Michelle, this has to stop, you know I'm getting married."

Forcefully pushing Carson away, Michelle yells, "Yes, I know but I don't understand why?"

"What do you mean you don't understand why?" Carson asked.

Snapping back sharply, "I guess what I don't understand is, why her and not me?"

Exhibiting a lack of concern for Michelle's feelings, "Do you really need to ask?" Carson said.

"I mean really, what is it? What made you love her over me? Is she prettier than me, smarter than me, what does she have that I don't Carson?" Michelle asked.

Believing Michelle was unworthy of a marriage proposal, in harsh terms, using brutal honesty, Carson said, "To be honest, she's everything you're not. I mean for Christ's sake, you just straight up told a bold face lie to my parent's in the house of the Lord to try and hook up with me. To me, that's a problem."

Punching Carson in the chest, through streaming tears, "So, I'm good enough for you to sleep with but not to marry? Is that what you're trying to say?" Michelle raged.

Unphased by Michelle's rant, "You seriously need to calm down and lower your voice. We were just having fun baby, you said you knew that and was fine with it. Now all of a sudden, you trying to get all serious on me, I don't think so. Check it, Michelle, you are a part of my past and Scarlett, my bride, is a part of my future." Carson said.

"How dare you, you son of a -." Michelle cried.

Taking a dangerous step close towards Michelle, Carson demanded, "Hey, you better watch yourself Michelle and I mean that. It's one thing to disrespect the church but when you start getting ready to disrespect my mother, we got a whole new set of problems and me getting married won't be one of them."

"Can't you see I just want to be with you? Can't you see I'm trying to keep you from making the biggest mistake of your life?" Michelle pleaded.

"Mistake?" Carson scoffed.

"Yeah, mistake. Carson, you don't love her, you can't, if you're still messing around with me." Michelle replied.

"And so you think I love you?" Carson asked laughing. "See, that's where you females mess up, y'all equate sex with love. For us, it can just be sex with no emotional attachment whatsoever. And you're wrong, I do love Scarlett. In fact, I love her very much and she's going to be my wife."

"You are the worst of the worst Carson Montgomery." Michelle criticized.

"Yeah but you were just trying to get all up in the worst of the worst." Carson replied.

"Oh yeah, about that." Walking seductively towards Carson. "You said we were just having fun, huh? You say she's everything I'm not. Well, let me ask you this. Will you love her so when she can't," whispering the rest into Carson's ear.

Feeling his knees buckle, "Good God, I reckon," Carson hollers biting his fist.

Satisfied with herself, Michelle stood with an open stance, hands on her hips and her elbows were widespread with pride, "That's what I thought."

Looking at the cross on the podium, Carson prays in his heart, pleading, *"Lord forgive me for I know not what I do. You heard what she said, what's a brother to do?"*

Chapter 2

"Who does this?" Minta Watson huffs in disgust walking in front of the rest of the family.

"Calm down Minta; I'm sure there's a perfectly good explanation." George defended.

Struggling with her luggage, "I will not calm down George, this is a travesty. First of all, who forgets to pick up their soon to be in-laws? If that wasn't bad enough, you and I both know this church does everything in excellence and they didn't see fit to send a driver or someone to pick us up from the airport. Not to mention, no one is here to greet us as we've had to arrange for our own transportation here. So no, I WILL NOT calm down until I find out what's going on around here. This is not how I want to start the week off that my daughter will be getting married."

Waving off his wife, George replies, "Oh Minta, give it a rest. I'm sure there's a lot going on around here in preparation for OUR daughter's wedding."

"Is there a perfectly good explanation as to why no one around here answers their phones? Why have a phone if you're not going to answer it, Jesus. Is there a good explanation as to why we're here at their church and no one is here to receive us?" Minta lamented.

Grabbing her last bag, the biggest from the van, Scarlett expressed, "Oh my God, mom please. Dad is right, I'm sure there's a reason Carson didn't show up at the airport but we're here now. I'm going to go and see if I can find someone who can tell me what's going on."

Handling her luggage as well as her husband roughly, Minta lashed out, "You want me to calm down but I tell you the truth, something in my spirit is telling me something isn't right. Something is off. I'm telling you George, this doesn't feel right to me."

Chuckling, "Your spirit huh? That's them day old collard greens you ate last night. Those same ones you refused to throw out like I told you. But no, you didn't want them to go to waste and now you think your spirit is trying to tell you something. I think you might need some Maalox."

"Shut up George." Minta snapped back with folded arms.

"Dad, you are crazy man. Mom, how about you take a seat here for a minute." Reaching into his bag, pulling out a bottled water, "Here, take a drink of this." Cole offered laughing.

"Oh, thank God, you guys are here." Carson shouts running inside in a frenzy.

"Yeah, we're here. No thanks to you." Minta scolded.

Attempting to greet his future mother-in-law proved to be slightly difficult given Minta's closed off body posture. Moving along to George and Cole, Carson found a small bit of comfort with the Watson men.

Making a clear observation, "Hey, wait a minute, where's Scarlett?" Carson asked looking around for his bride-to-be.

"She went looking for someone to tell us what's going on around here. Speaking of, where were you man and why weren't you answering your phone? We had to get our own transportation here man. What happened to you?" Cole asked grilling Carson.

Glancing at the cross again on the podium, swallowing hard, tried to explain, 'Man, you ain't even going to believe this."

"Probably not." Minta mumbled.

Ignoring Minta's comment, Carson attempted to justify his actions, "First of all, my phone died and I didn't have my charger. Then, I was on my way to the airport and I got tied up in a big and I mean big 'ole jam. Man, if you could have seen it, it was an amazing sight."

Standing up and easing closer to Carson, "Hmm, that's funny because we didn't see any accidents on the way here in the transportation we arranged for ourselves." Minta sharply replied.

Placing his arms around a boiling over Minta, George stepped in between Carson and his wife.

Grateful for George's gesture, Carson nervously moved over and said, "I'm pretty sure I didn't take the same route as you guys. When I got to the airport and couldn't find you all nor could I call, my heart sank. I didn't know what to do. I am so, so very sorry; I hope you can forgive me. This is not how I wanted you guys to start your week here with us. I sincerely apologize for the mix-up."

Staring at Minta, "We accept your apology and all is forgiven son." George replies.

Running towards Carson squealing, Scarlett and Carson embrace as he twirls his soon to be bride around in excitement.

Upon placing Scarlett back on the ground, after a quick kiss to the lips, Scarlett playfully swats Carson asking, "Where have you been and why couldn't I get in touch with you?"

"I'm so glad to see you too, Scarlett, my heart, my love. I'm so sorry I was late to the airport and missed picking you all up. I was just telling your family here, I got caught up in something I didn't expect and my phone died." Carson said, looking up at the alter again.

"Okay...whatever that means Carson, you're saying you got caught up, you mean like in a traffic jam?" Scarlett asked.

"Exactly, see baby you get me and you understand me but let's not talk about that anymore. Let me look at you at," Carson says twirling Scarlett around again stomping his feet in unison. "Good God

I reckon, girl, you look good to me. Boy, I'm a lucky man."

Giggling and smiling from ear-to-ear, the light rose tint in Scarlett's cheeks showed up brightly as she replied, "Thank you honey, you look good too. I'm so happy to see you. Now, I knew there was a reason. I wouldn't believe for a second, you'd ever forget about me."

"Alright, alright, as much as I hate to break up this little love fest, can someone PLEASE tell me where I can get settled and ready for tonight's reception?" Minta bellowed.

"Yes honey, my mother's right, it was a long flight and I think we'd all like to take a breather and get freshened up, right Cole, right Dad?" Scarlett announced.

Speaking up at the same time, both Cole and George agreed.

"Yes sweetheart, that sounds great; I could use a little down time." George said.

"Yeah sis, I'm down with that." Cole replied.

"No problem, no problem at all. There's an area set up for each of you here on the grounds and then after tonight's reception, you all will be taken to where you'll be staying throughout the week." Carson instructed.

Gathering their luggage, preparing to leave, Cole shouts out, "Hey Carson, do you mind if I holler at you for a minute?"

Bringing Carson off to the side, Cole probes, "So what's the deal on some of these church girls man?"

"Oh, no brother, I'm about to be a married man. I don't know nothing about these girls. However, I will tell you this, you might think you're on the hunt prowling but beware because you just might get hunted down around here."

Gaining Cole and Carson's attention, the exceptionally loud clearing of Minta's throat worked. The squint of her eyes was familiar to Cole, he knew it was time to get moving.

"Alright man, I think we better get going, we don't want to get on mom's bad side." Cole remarked.

"Oh, there's a different one? I think I live on the bad one; I didn't realize there was a good side." Carson said.

Walking back towards the others Cole and Carson continued laughing and joking.

"Are we ready to go now?" Minta asked.

With downcast eyes, Carson answered, "Yes, yes, we are...will everyone, please follow me."

Chapter 3

"I wonder what's taking them so long to arrive." Regina said rolling her shoulders and glancing at the clock on the wall. "I hope they were pleased with their welcome gifts we prepared for them."

"Oh honey, stop worrying. Everything looks amazing. I'm sure they'll be here any minute now. Plus, for every minute they aren't here, I get to stand next to my beautiful wife and tell her how pretty she looks tonight." Bishop said.

Limos and expensive cars continued to circle the circular driveway as the hired valet drivers for the evening parked cars.

Twisting her ring, Regina smiled and said, "Thank you honey, I just want everything to be perfect. People are here and waiting and it seems to be taking them a really long time to show up. I hope everything is alright."

From corner to corner, everywhere the eyes could see, there was expensive décor and symbols of opulence; ice sculptures, tall tables for guests to gather, table linens and covered chairs with flickering candles on the tables with beautiful floral centerpieces.

Arm in arm, Carson escorts Scarlett into the full-swing welcoming reception with her family walking behind them.

"See look sweetheart, I told you not to worry, here they are now." Bishop announced.

Clusters of guests formed to feast their eyes upon the exquisiteness of the couple and the family that followed. Their indistinct chatter gave room to believe they approved of what they saw.

Scarlett, standing next to Carson illuminated the room all on her own but the two of them together electrified it.

Adorned in a stylish, off-the-shoulder dress complete with long, bell sleeves in a color that suggested Scarlett was everything a man could hope for. The strappy metallic sandals showcasing her tiny, manicured feet, bottomed her out. While her side-swept cascading curls complemented her look for the evening and topped her off. At her welcoming reception, Scarlett was as beautiful as her name and owned the room.

Rushing over to greet the Montgomery's, Regina beams with pride as she fawns over Scarlett.

The reunion of the two families proved to be bittersweet.

"Oh, hi First Lady Regina, it's so nice to see you again; I'm so happy to finally be here and everything looks wonderful." Scarlett said.

Touching Scarlett's face with her French-manicured hands, Regina said smiling, "That's my girl, just as lovely as ever. You look gorgeous. Did you all get settled in okay?"

Interrupting Scarlett's reply, Minta blurts out scoffing, "Yeah, no thanks to your son, Carson here."

"Minta!" George chastised sternly.

Smoothing down the front of her rhinestone suit, Regina said, "Minta, can you please repeat that? Run that by me again."

"With pleasure. Oh yes, we got settled, no thanks to Carson. 'Ole Sonny boy here, he didn't pick us up from the airport. Claims he got caught up in some traffic jam. Every last one of us tried calling. We called him, we called you, we tried everyone we could think of but we couldn't reach anyone. We had to arrange our own transportation here."

Locking eyes with Regina with grave concern, "Carson? What is she talking about, we left you here thinking you were on your way to pick them up, what happened?" Bishop asked.

Moving about, unable to stand still in one spot, Carson offered his explanation, "Bishop, please hear me out; I can explain. Like I told them earlier; I got caught up. Caught up in a big mess of an accident. I wish I hadn't but I did, and believe me, I'm so sorry it happened. Looking back, I probably should have gone a different route but by the time I realized it, it was already too late."

With darting glances at the Watson's, Bishop said, "Well family, I hate that happened to you all. It sounds like one of those freak of nature type things."

"Man, you can say that again, it was freaky for sure." Carson echoed.

Ignoring Carson's comment, Bishop continued, "However, I'm so glad you all are here and now we can officially kick off Carson and Scarlett's wedding week. If you're excited to be here, let the church say, Amen."

The entire clan shouts Amen, except for Minta.

"Minta!" George rebuked.

With a hard, obvious swallow and a slow response through clenched teeth, Minta replied, "Amen."

Clasping his hands together, Bishop said, "Good, alright. Now that everyone's here; I have something I want to say."

Interjecting with a step forward, Minta said, "Yes, and as a matter of fact, I do too."

Gently pulling her back close to his side, George firmly stated, "Oh no you don't. Go ahead Bishop."

"I just want to say, it gives me great pleasure to kick off this celebration for this lovely couple. Back during the Bible days, they celebrated weddings as week-long events and we intend to do the same. We are so delighted to be welcoming Scarlett into our family. I've personally counseled these two young people and I believe they are ready to enter into the covenant relationship of marriage." Bishop Montgomery proclaimed.

Uniformed servers dressed in black and white passed hors d'oeuvres and drinks from their carrying trays around to both families as well as other invited guests in attendance.

Even the uninvited are served as Michelle enters the elaborate affair, the sophisticated workmanship of the church's event planning team.

"Crab puff please." Michelle said stuffing the miniature morsel into her mouth as she surveyed the room.

"I'd like to echo what my husband has said. I'm just so excited Carson has chosen Scarlett to be his wife. I mean Minta, who knew that when we contacted you to help us with the church we'd be here today?" Regina said.

Under mumbled breath, Minta responded, "Yeah really, who knew? Thanks for the reminder."

In an attempt to calm his mother, Cole reaches for another crab puff from the silver polished tray passing them.

"Well, I promise, this is only the beginning, our staff has planned an awesome itinerary. Let's see, we have the golf tournament coming up, the concert, the comedy show, the vineyard, I mean they have all sorts of things planned leading up to the big day." Bishop declared.

Scarlett's soft eyes sparkled with an inner glow as she said, "Thank you so much Bishop and First Lady Regina for putting all of this together. You guys are the best and I'm so grateful because without you two, there would be no him and I'm so happy to be marrying the man of my dreams."

Moving closer to Scarlett and grabbing her hands, Regina looked her directly in the face and said, "You are family now, stop it with the First Lady Regina stuff. I want you to call me Mama Montgomery from now on."

Hugging and embracing one another, Scarlett tears up slightly, "Oh First Lady, I mean, Mama Montgomery, you have no idea how much that means to me. Thank you."

Pointing towards Regina and Scarlett, the two most important women in his life smiling, Carson kisses Regina on the cheek and grabs Scarlett by the hand. "I love you baby and I can't wait to make you my wife." Carson whispers softly.

Gushing, Scarlett leans in closer to Carson, "I love you too baby."

Moving in about the happy couple, watching their every move, Michelle frowns and pouts upon hearing Carson profess his love for Scarlett.

"That's right son, cherish her, love on her like Christ loves the church. Hold her tight and never let her go." Regina admonished

Patting Carson on the back, "That's right son, I want you to be true to her. Never stop loving her, always treat her like your bride. I want you to treasure the jewel Scarlett is to you and this family." Bishop instructed.

Off in the near distance, Michelle winks and waves at Carson.

Notwithstanding a notice from Minta.

"Well, here again, as my husband has said, we look forward to this week. This place is packed, people are here to celebrate this beautiful couple and we are so grateful. We have family and friends who've traveled from near and far to share in this special time for our family. I love you all now let's go and have a great night, let's mingle with our guests. To Scarlett and Carson."

Raised glasses respond to Regina and the two families speak in unison, "To Scarlett and Carson."

Everyone except a bothered and clearly unhappy Minta.

Chapter 4

"Outstanding event tonight honey. I think everyone had a great time, don't you? I tell you one thing; you are indeed the hostess with the mostess. You worked this room tonight baby girl." Bishop said kissing Regina's hand.

"Yeah but not everyone." Regina alleged.

"Did I miss something because from what I could tell, everyone in this room seemed to be having a blast and enjoying themselves. You say that like you're referring to someone in particular." Bishop suggested.

"Eugene, I've been telling you for weeks now to schedule an appointment at the eye doctor because Ray Charles, Stevie Wonder, and Helen Keller combined could see that Minta was not having a good time tonight. She seems different this time, something seems off with her, like something's not right." Regina contended.

"Hmm, I just figured she was tired from traveling." Bishop replied.

Turning the remaining lights off in the reception area, "Now Eugene, you and I both know, Minta has traveled out here many times before and I've never seen her like she was tonight. She travels all over the country on a regular basis. I don't think it was the traveling." Regina scoffed.

Offering Regina to take a seat next to him, Bishop Montgomery grabbed Regina's hand and proposed an answer, "Could it be she's stressed out because her only daughter is getting married? You see honey, we don't have daughters,

; we have three sons so we'll be gaining daughters. She may be feeling like she's losing hers."

In a slight nod of agreement, Regina reluctantly gave consideration to her husband, "I guess she could be. I mean, Scarlett will be living out here with us but it would seem to me, she would be a happy stressed...but she's not."

"Well honey, I wouldn't read too much into it." Bishop answered.

"How can I not? You don't seem to reading enough into it. This is important to me Eugene. I don't want anything to ruin this wedding. Not even the mother of the bride." Regina yelled.

"Honey, calm down. Hey listen, I'm on your side here. You know what, it's been a long day, I thought maybe you'd be ready to head home since we're the last ones here. However, if you need to talk this through, let's talk about it. If there's one thing I can see; I can see this is really weighing on you." Bishop expressed.

Lowering her gaze from her husband's loving and concerned eyes, Regina expressed, "Eugene, this really is weighing on me, it really is. I need to ask you something and I need for you to be completely honest with me."

Squishing his eyebrows together, Bishop said, "I'm always honest with you honey."

Shaking her head, "No, no you're not and especially when it comes to our sons. I think we hide the truth from ourselves when it comes to them. Too many times, we both need eye appointments when it comes to them because we tend to turn blinded eyes." Regina confessed.

In a dismissive laugh and tone, Bishop replied, "Oh Regina, c'mon. That's an extreme characterization don't you think?"

Snapping back sharply, breaking their hand holding, "No Eugene, you c'mon. You think this is funny? You think I'm joking and going extreme huh? Well, let me ask you something. Do you think our son, Carson is ready to get married? Is that boy really ready to be somebody's husband?"

"Regina, why are you yelling? We are the only two people left, it's just you and me baby." Bishop explained.

"I'm yelling because not only can you not see, you apparently can't hear either. I need you to hear what I'm saying Eugene and it doesn't seem like I'm getting through to you." Regina hollered.

Taking a moment to carefully consider his words, Bishop started, "Regina, seriously, is anybody ever really ready to get married? Even those who think they are have no idea what's at stake and what they're in for."

"Listen, I get that but I just can't shake this feeling I have." Regina replied. Tapping her foot with crossed arms across her chest, "Why was Carson late picking up the Watson's, huh...answer me that?"

"Regina, sweetheart, you heard the answer the boy gave. Things got out of his control. None of us can control the traffic and the accidents that may happen on the road, honey." Bishop answered.

"Yeah, I heard what he said but for some reason, his answer did not bear witness with me Eugene. And like I said, if you'd be honest, I don't think it did with you either." Regina surmised.

Pulling Regina into himself, "Honey, I think the wedding preparations has you stretched too thin and things are starting to get to you. Let's go home and get some rest, we have a full day planned for tomorrow." Bishop Montgomery whispered.

Pushing back, Regina made her intentions known, "Eugene, stop trying to handle me. I'm very well aware of what's going on and what's being planned because I planned them. Whether you want to be honest or not, based on how I feel; I don't want any of Carson's shenanigans to ruin Scarlett. She's too good of a girl for that to happen."

"Honey listen to me." Bishop urged.

"No, you listen to me Eugene. Carson knows he can't take over the church if he isn't married but if he isn't ready, as his parents, we owe it to him and Scarlett for that fact to do something about it." Regina expressed.

Stroking his silvery goatee, "You're asking for honesty, right? I think I know where all this is coming from. You think he hooked up with that girl who sent us on a wild goose chase earlier, don't you?" Bishop asked.

Throwing her hands up in the air, "Don't you?" Regina yelled. See that's what I'm talking about Eugene, we're both thinking it but had I not said anything, we probably wouldn't be discussing it. But now that we are, don't we have a responsibility here? You know, there's a story in the bible that haunts me often when it comes to our sons."

Sitting down again, Bishop asked, "And which story might that be?"

"The story of Eli and his two sons. Eli was a sincere and devout man of God, just like you, Eugene. But those hard-headed boys of his." Regina recounted.

Laughing heartily, "Regina, are you seriously comparing our boys to Eli's?"

"Yes, yes I am. His sons worked in ministry and so do ours. Eli was old but that didn't stop him from hearing about what his children were doing and you know about all of the stuff we hear about Carson." Regina explained.

Pleading and making a case, Bishop grabbed Regina by her shoulders, "Listen to me honey, we're not getting any younger, in fact, we're starting to get up there like Eli. Carson is next in line to lead this ministry; his legacy demands it of him. Honey, you and I both know, he's being groomed to be the next leader of this ministry. The grooming started the day he was born, sweetheart, just like it did with me. If he's not ready, then he needs to get ready and that's all I have to say about that. He needs to get ready." Bishop said.

Making a plea of her own, "What do we do to get him ready Eugene, he's getting married in a few days. If you didn't notice, the bride and her family arrived today and Carson couldn't even pick them up on time." Regina replied.

"I'll talk to him honey." Bishop offered.

Stepping backwards to pick up a bible from one of the pews, "I need you to do more than talk to him Eugene." Holding up the bible in front of Bishop, "You see, that's all Eli did, he talked and his sons still didn't listen. They continued to disobey and God was not pleased. He sent judgment to Eli's house, severe destruction came upon the house of Eli." Shaking her head slowly, "Oh my heavenly Father, I don't want that to happen to us, give us a chance to make things right." Regina sniveled.

With outstretched arms, Bishop walked closer, "My dearest Regina, please come here and listen to me for a minute. Yes, Carson has some issues but don't we all. He's no different than any other person out there. We're all humans and with that, we're bound to fail. However, as believers, we all have a fail proof switch deep down within us, the Holy Spirit, to help us. The funny thing is, even as believers, we still fail sometimes. The only difference in some of us is that we know how to allow the perfect work of the Holy Spirit to work within us and mortify the deeds of our flesh. You see, when the Holy Spirit has room, He takes it and he examines the root, while we're out here looking at the fruit. The problem comes in with the pruning process, it's not easy and sometimes, people stop the pruning process before the work is done. It's easier to flip that switch back off. Carson is going to submit to the process and let the Holy Spirit do its job." Bishop declared.

"I guess you think you're a preacher now, do I look like I need you to give me a sermon? Look, I don't need you to be my pastor right now. What I need is for you to be my husband and a father to our children. Even if we are to go with the little sermonette you just gave, we have to admit and be honest that Carson has some bad fruit that needs to be dealt with." Regina exclaimed.

Leaning away, "Oh wow, you aren't going to let this go, are you? This thing has really gotten a hold of you, huh?" Bishop said.

Regina's rapid eye blinking led into a wide-eyed look at Bishop Montgomery, "As it should be to you too and that's all I've been trying to get you to understand. You should be feeling the same way as I do about this and it doesn't seem like you are. I don't need you to just talk to him. I need you to knock some sense into him if you have to. Using your words, get a pair of pruning shears if need be. I'm so serious Eugene, do whatever it takes, get through to him." Regina argued.

"Honey, honey, honey, I hear you and I promise, I'll deal with Carson. I'll even drop kick him if I have to." Bishop said demonstrating a drop kick.

"Here I am trying to be serious and you're trying to make me laugh, how is that even right?" Regina asked smiling.

"There's that beautiful smile; I see it worked. Now, you just asked me a whole lot of questions and I have one for you." Bishop said.

"What is it Eugene?"

"Can we FINALLY go home woman?"

The sounds of their combined laughter bought them closer, hugging and kissing each other in a shared surrender of the conversation at hand.

"Yes, sweetheart, we can go home. What are we going to do when we get there?" Regina asked with parting lips.

"Oh, I have an idea or two." Breaking out into a song, "I'll give myself away. I'll give myself away, so you, can use me."

Both with smiles across their faces, Regina grabs Bishop's hand, "Sing it Bishop Montgomery, I like the sounds of that. Let's go home."

Chapter 5

"What a beautiful day to host this golf tournament, huh?" George said. "Are we the first ones to arrive?

"It sure is daddy, I couldn't agree with you more, it's a perfect Fall day." Scarlett replied. "It looks like we're early, you and I were always the early birds. Let's get some breakfast while we wait."

The dry October air mixed with the sea breeze from the Pacific Ocean against the sunny backdrop made for perfect weather.

The whirring sound of the off-white golf carts buzzed by along the well-manicured paths leading to the club house. George and Scarlett stood and watched in admiration of the game of golf.

They'd participated in tournaments together before but this one was different, this one was special.

"So Scarlett, are you ready to whip up on the Montgomery's and show them how the Watson's roll the rock?" George asked motioning a putting swing.

"Oh, you better believe I am. For a few more days, I'm still a Watson, I'm not a Montgomery yet." Scarlett said laughing.

Nearly cringing and looking away, George said, "Scarlett Montgomery. I don't know if I'll ever get used to saying that."

In a light bubbly voice, Scarlett stood behind her father and placed her arms around his neck, "Yes daddy, that's going to be my name and I'm sure you'll get used to it because I plan on being married for a loooonnnngggg time." Scarlett expressed.

Releasing a heavy sigh, "Wow, I just can't seem to believe my baby girl is getting married. My goodness, where has the time gone? Feels like yesterday I was bringing you home from the hospital. Pushing you on the swings, singing made up Scarlett songs, tucking you in and reading bedtime stories." George said as his voice tapered off becoming somewhat emotional.

Taking notice to George's changed demeanor, "Daddy, are you alright?" Scarlett asked.

Searching for the right words, "Uh, yeah, baby, I think um, you know, I uh, I've been dealing with this here, um condition." George announced.

A rise in Scarlett's voice as she rushed by her father's side, "Condition? What kind of condition and why am I just hearing about this?" Scarlett inquired.

With the straightest face, George confessed, "Yeah, I um, I started having symptoms right after Carson proposed to you."

"Daddy, you're scaring me. Does mom know about this, does Cole? How serious is this, what are your doctors saying to you? Speak up, tell me what's going on." Scarlett shouted.

Taking in a deep breath, "I wasn't aware such a condition even existed but after talking to a few buddies of mine. I realized I was suffering from the Father-Marrying-Off-His-First-Child-And-She's-A-Girl-Disease." George admitted.

Playfully swatting George and crossing her hands across her chest, Scarlett yelled, "Daddy, you had me scared to death over here. I'm all nervous thinking I'm about to lose my daddy and here you are playing with my emotions."

Initiating a hug with Scarlett while laughing, "I'm sorry sweetheart; I couldn't resist. I was just joking around with you. However, as you can see, it doesn't feel good when you feel like you're about to lose someone you love." George affirmed.

"But daddy, you aren't going to lose me; I'm always going to be your little girl." Scarlett said softly.

"Yeah, maybe to you and me, you'll always be that but for crying out loud Scarlett, you're about to become someone's wife." George replied.

"While that's true, I promise you it won't change the relationship you and I share." Scarlett said looking into her bag. "See look."

"And what do we have here, what is this sweetheart?" George asked.

"I was waiting for the right time to give this to you and this seems like just as good a time as any." Passing the gift to George, "Open it." Scarlett insisted.

Opening the gift, George pauses, the intensity of the emotions he feels overwhelms him, but in a good way.

Taking the gift from George, Scarlett opens it up, "I can see you have a little something in your eye so let me read it for you. It says, daddy, you'll always be the first man I've ever loved. Thank you for being there every step of the way. Love Scarlett."

Scarlett gifted her father a pair of socks, the print on the left foot read, "By Your Side," and the print on the right foot read, "Every Step of the Way."

"That's beautiful baby; you've always been such a sweet girl. That's very thoughtful of you. I think I'll wear these on your special day." George said.

"Well, you will be by my said on that day and this is something you'll always have unless they turn into some of the hole-y socks you have at home." Scarlett joked.

"Even if they do, I'll wear them proudly, holes and all." George replied.

"I just wanted you to know how much I love, appreciate, and respect you." Scarlett professed.

Pretending his allergies are acting up instead of becoming emotional, "Is there such a thing as Fall allergies?" George said smiling.

"Allergies huh? I see you tough guy. Let's see if you can handle this." Scarlett said offering George a handkerchief.

Reaching for the handkerchief, "Of course I can handle it; I can handle anything you throw my way. I'm just going to grab this kerchief, you know, just in case." George said laughing.

Sitting down in front of George, Scarlett explains, "The way I see it, having you as my dad; I feel there isn't anything I can't do. I want you to know, you raised me well and I truly appreciate that. Now, come Saturday, I'll be able to walk down the aisle as the luckiest woman in the world. I'll have the first man I've ever loved leading me to the man I've fallen in love with."

"Stop it now Scarlett, you're taking me too fast, too soon, I believe my condition is starting to flare up." George exclaimed.

"Do you remember when I asked you to go dress shopping with us?" Scarlett asked.

"Boy, do I. I couldn't believe you asked me that, I didn't even know men were allowed in those stores. I tried to get out of it by saying, honey, I'm sure you ladies will find the perfect dress." George said laughing.

Reflecting back on the memory, Scarlett smiled, "Yes, you did but I insisted."

"Well, you've always been a persistent little thing." George replied.

"I knew I'd know when to say yes to the dress from the look on your face and I was right. Out of all the dresses I tried on, when I saw your face in "the one" and we both teared up; I knew it was my dress and now I can't wait to see Carson's face." Scarlett said.

George's swelled chest and quivering chin confirmed the song in his heart for his daughter, "That is a moment I'll cherish for the rest of my life, thank you for insisting."

"I love you daddy."

"I love you more sweetheart, more than you know. Seeing you grow up into this amazing woman has been my greatest joy. Now I know a little about how God must feel about us. His love for us is everlasting. You and your brother have been the best lesson to teach me about being a child of God. Like our Heavenly Father, He desires for us to reach our greatest potential and that's the same I want for you." George said.

Tearing up, Scarlett gushed, "Oh daddy."

"It's true sweetheart, just as God is exceedingly glad we are His children; I'm overjoyed to have you as my daughter. Now, since we're here having this conversation, as your dad, I have to know. Do you think Carson is the right man for you and are you happy?" George questioned.

Feeling a lightness in her chest and a warmth spreading through her body, Scarlett quickly replied with a resounding, "Yes. Yes, daddy I do think he is the right man for me. I love him very much and he makes me happy." Scarlett acknowledged. "We've never really talked about this before but what I want to know from you is, do you think he's the right man for me?"

Displaying a distant, unfocused smile, "It's not about what I think Scarlett. Do I have my own opinions, yes, but this is a decision you need to be confident in. I'm not the one marrying him, you are, which means, you take all of what comes along with being married to Carson Montgomery." George stated.

Scarlett's lips pressed together in a slight grimace, "I respect that and I wish more people felt like you."

Family and friends dressed in golf attire began entering the club house.

"I guess people are starting to gather for the tournament." George observed.

"Yeah, it looks that way. I've really enjoyed this time with you this morning daddy." Scarlett replied.

Placing a kiss to Scarlett's cheek, George stood saying, "Me too."

Cautiously interrupting the father-daughter moment, "Hey, good morning, there you are sunshine. How are you two this morning?" Carson asked greeting Scarlett and George.

"I'm fantastic, just spending a little time with my daddy before we whip up on the Montgomery's this morning." Scarlett boasted.

"Not a chance, you must not know about how the Montgomery's own these links out here in Vino." Carson said joking.

Standing tall with his hands on his hips and looking around, "Vino, California. This is where my baby's going to be living?" George said.

Sharing a look and winking at Scarlett, Carson's enthusiasm burst forth, "Yes sir, as Mrs. Carson Eugene Montgomery IV and I can't wait."

"Well hold on there Mr. I-Can't-Wait. There's something I need to tell you." George cautioned.

"Okay, what is it George?" Carson asked.

"Carson, now, I know you are waiting in line to become the next pastor of your family's church but I have a position I'd like to appoint you to." George revealed.

Belting out a quick-high pitched laughter, Scarlett asked, "What are you talking about daddy? What kind of position do you have for Carson?"

Holding a finger up to Scarlett and looking directly at Carson, "Do you believe my daughter, my only daughter, Scarlett is the right woman for you?" George probed.

Being hyper-aware of the reactions of those surrounding him, Scarlett and her father, Carson answered, "Yes I do sir, indeed I do. As a matter of fact, I'm a blessed man that she would love me the way she does."

George's high chin and exposed neck looked over at Carson, "Well, in that case, I hereby appoint you the President and Chief Operating Officer of Scarlett's fan club. Hear me when I say, your responsibilities will include loving my daughter and keeping her safe. I will expect you to willingly put my daughter's well-being above anything else and ANYONE else. Do you get what I'm saying to you son and do you accept?" George demanded.

Swallowing hard but with a smile, "Yes sir, I follow you and I gladly accept the position and its responsibilities." Carson accepted.

Placing his firm hand on Carson's shoulder, "You say you feel she's the right one for you, now you go and be the right one for her. You hear me?" George declared.

"Loud and clear sir." Carson said.

"The teams are starting to form, come on let's get ready to go." Scarlett said.

Grabbing his things, "Hold on you two, I have one more thing to say to Carson. Carson, you said you heard me and if you don't do what I'm asking, I'll have to fire you."

Repeating back George's words, "Fire me?" Carson asked.

Looking directly at Carson, while retrieving a small pocket lighter and striking it, "Yes and I'm not talking about the kinds of firings and terminations I do at my bank." George replied.

Chapter 6

"Wow, what an amazing golf course. The courses out here are much different than the ones in Jordon, I may have to come visit you Scarlett just so I can come play golf." George said adjusting his golf glove.

"I know daddy, being out there on the links it's like you get to see where wine country meets the Pacific coast." Scarlett said.

"Speaking of wine, I particularly enjoyed the free wine tastings at each hole. Now that was impressive." Cole expressed.

Rolling her eyes at her brother, "Is that all you enjoyed Cole? I mean, it's such a beautiful day and the views of the ocean from every hole were simply breathtaking." Scarlett replied.

"Not as breathtaking as you sweetheart." Carson chimed in. Greeting everyone with enthusiasm, Carson went around high-fiving the foursome, "Team Watson," he shouted.

Cole, Scarlett, George, and Sherry with raised hands harmoniously replied, "Team Watson."

Sherry Watson, Scarlett's cousin, her maid of honor surprised the family by showing up a few days before scheduled and a welcomed surprise it was as Sherry had to step in and play for said Team Watson.

Sherry's mother, Juanita had a strained relationship with her brother, George, however, despite the discord, Sherry however, always maintained a close and loving relationship with her family.

Sherry herself was also engaged to be married and would be tying the knot around the Christmas holidays.

Being a hospitable and caring host, "I think everything is just about ready in the clubhouse for lunch. Mother told me on the course that you guys are in for a surprise with the menu. Let me go and check." Carson said.

"I can't wait to see the scores, to see who won the tournament." Cole said.

"Well, I don't really care what they have planned on their menu because we already ate the Montgomery's for lunch out on the links." George said laughing.

"Uncle George, you are a mess." Sherry said. Grabbing Scarlett by the hand, Sherry asked, "Scarlett, can I speak to you for a minute?"

Walking over to a more private space, Sherry stood facing Scarlett and said, "Um, so I see it's a good thing I showed up here this morning, what happened to your mom? Why isn't she here, is she feeling alright?"

Shrugging her shoulders and in an uncertain tone, "I don't know cousin, she's been acting strange since we got here. And you're right, good thing you did show up, she was supposed to be on my team, literally and figuratively but I seriously don't know."

"Well at least you don't have to deal with the inconsistencies of my mother; I'd take yours over mine any day." Sherry said sneering.

Waving her hands in the hair, "Can we please change the subject from our mothers? What I want to know is, how did you manage to get here so early and I not know about it?" Scarlett asked.

"That handsome fiancé you have there, arranged everything, my dear, sweet cousin. I called him and told him I wanted to surprise you by arriving a few days early and he told me not to worry, that he'd take care of everything...and he did." Sherry admitted.

Holding onto Sherry's hand longer than necessary, "He's quite the guy, hearing that makes me love him even more and oh my goodness, I'm so happy you're here, so glad to have my big cousin here with me. The rest of the bridal party won't be here until the end of the week so it's nice to have you here enjoying all of this with me. Will Glenn come early too?"

Glenn Palmer, an up and coming attorney, on the fast track to becoming partner at his law firm met Sherry during a deposition, where she was opposing counsel.

The scales of justice tipped in Sherry's favor but not without also winning the heart of Glenn.

"I don't think so, he's wrapping up a case, but who knows, he may decide to surprise me, there seems to be a lot of that going on around here." Sherry said smiling. "Can you believe it Scarlett, these are the days, the moments we dreamed of as little girls. Do you remember how we used to play with our dolls pretending to be married? Then as we got older we'd talk about falling in love, getting married, having children, and now, it's all finally happening."

The two women squealed in utter excitement at the realization of their childhood hopes and dreams.

Making her way through the crowds, Regina searched until she found Scarlett talking with Sherry.

"I don't mean to interrupt you two but Scarlett, honey, I want to show you something before we sit down for lunch and have the awards ceremony." Regina said.

Taking a quick glance at Sherry, Scarlett stood up to greet Regina, "Go ahead Scarlett, I'll meet you inside." Sherry submitted.

Mouthing, "Thank-you," to Sherry, Regina smiled and escorted Scarlett inside the clubhouse. "So, I have something I want to show you." Regina said.

"What is it, what do you want to show me?" Scarlett asked.

Offering light touches while speaking to Scarlett, "As you know, you were here two weeks ago, for your engagement photos, right? I hope you don't mind but I took the liberty of choosing the best-looking ones and my plan is to reveal my choices at each event, starting now." Regina explained removing a satin covering from a large frame.

Scarlett's chest hitched with emotion as she absorbed the enormity of the kind gesture from Regina, coupled with the beauty of the photograph, along with the image of seeing herself with the love of her life. In that moment, it was all too much to handle.

"Do you like it?" Regina asked.

"Do I like it; I love it, this is..." Scarlett said crying as her voice tapered off.

Shedding a tear of her own, Regina smiled and said, "I'm glad you like it sweetheart. You have no idea, I have so much planned for you this week, this is just the beginning."

"Really, you've done so much already, I don't know if I can handle much more." Scarlett said.

Scores of people walked in as the two women embraced.

"There you are; I was wondering where you went; I was looking for you. I think everyone is ready to eat, especially after that beat down Team Montgomery put on Team Watson." Carson cheered.

Coming up behind him, George offered, "Yeah, we'll see about that."

Outside changing his shoes, Cole slipped his golf shoes off and into his bag before heading inside.

"I saw you out there on the golf course today." Michelle said.

"Oh yeah." Cole replied.

"Yeah and you were looking good too." Michelle said.

"Is that right?" Cole asked.

Moving in closer, Michelle pulled a chair up next to Cole, "So tell me, why aren't you inside with everyone else?" Michelle inquired.

"I'm about to go inside but I wanted to change my shoes first. Is that alright with you?" Cole asked.

"It's perfectly fine with me because it gives me an opportunity to finally be able to talk to you, Team Watson." Michelle replied.

"That's right, Team Watson all the way baby." Cole said smiling.

Inching in a little closer, with a tilt of her head, "So the bride is your sister huh? She's a real pretty girl; I can see why Carson chose her." Michelle said.

"Pretty ain't even the word to describe my sister, my sister is straight up gorgeous and Carson, that's my man, he's lucky to have someone like her. Scarlett, she's a great person and I'm happy for her." Cole said.

Licking her lips, having an opened body posture, and stroking her elongated neck, "I think we should hang out later, what do you think?" Michelle asked.

Showing a lack of discernment and an inability to read Michelle's cues, "Oh you mean all of us as a group after this evening's event, are you going?" Cole said.

Not beating around the bush, Michelle expressed, "Oh yes, I'll be there but I was thinking more of a smaller group, like you and I."

Becoming suddenly still with a stiffened posture, "Oh okay, I think that can be arranged. I'm going to go inside but I'll look for you tonight." Cole said standing.

"You do that because if you don't I'll be looking for you." Michelle solicited.

Chapter 7

"Hey mom, I stopped by to check on you. What happened, you missed the tournament this morning. Are you feeling alright?" Cole asked.

With an opened bible in her lap and speaking barely above a whisper, Minta replied, "I'm alright son, what are you up to? How was the tournament?"

Bouncing from one foot to the other, "You missed it Mom, the tournament was amazing and of course you know Team Watson brought the trophy home, we won." Cole exclaimed.

"Oh yeah, how did that happen, who filled in for me?" Minta asked.

Slam-dunking his trash into the barrel next to him, "You won't believe this but Sherry showed up. She flew in this morning to surprise Scarlett, she surprised us all actually. I'm just glad she knew how to play golf." Cole said laughing.

"That was nice, I didn't think she was supposed to get here until later this week." Minta recalled.

"That's what I'm trying to tell you, she got here earlier than expected. Did you hear anything I said, are you sure you're okay?" Cole asked.

"I'm sorry son; I guess I got carried away in my own thoughts, I'm halfway paying attention to what you're saying, tell me again what you said. You said, Sherry showed up early? Did Glenn come with her, did that trifling mother of hers show up too?" Minta scoffed.

For years, Minta and George tried to save Sherry's mother, Juanita but all of their attempts were all for naught. Notorious for focusing on people's flaws rather than their attributes, Minta would constantly berate any progress Juanita would make. She rarely offered any praise on the small steps she did make. Minta always believed Juanita could do better, if she really wanted to. Truth be told, Minta harbored hidden resentment towards the siblings. She was upset with George for his many attempts despite her multiple warnings. In addition, she was upset with his sister for not accepting their assistance. Intolerant towards giving Juanita yet another chance, the last chance was the last time they saw her.

Collapsing onto the chair next to Minta, "That's it, I want to know what's going on with you. You've been acting strange since we got here. We are here for Scarlett's wedding, are you even happy she's getting married, MOB, mother-of-the-bride?" Cole asked.

Slamming her bible closed shut, "Yes, I'm happy she's getting married; I'm just not happy who she's marrying. You called me a M-O-B well right now I'm feeling like the MOB, I feel like tearing up some stuff." Minta shouted.

Cole's flinched head, snapped back quickly, "What are you talking about, so now you have a problem with Carson? From what I can tell, he's a good guy." Counting on his fingers, "Is he overindulged, yes. Spoiled, yes. Feels untouchable, yes but when you look past all of that, he's a really good guy, righteous even." Cole conveyed.

"Righteous my a--." Minta mocked.

"Mom?" Cole shouted.

Minta was never one to curse, she lived her life under a strict moral code and she believed those who used those words did so due to their limited vocabulary.

Grabbing the sides of her head, "Oh Lord Jesus, this thing here is getting the best of me." Minta screamed aloud.

"But why though? I don't understand why you now all of a sudden have a problem with Scarlett marrying Carson. It doesn't make sense." Cole questioned.

Snapping back sharply, "I ain't never liked it, I've always had a problem with it. I'm telling you Cole, I just don't like what I see in him." Minta admitted.

"But you gave them your blessing." Cole described.

Minta's foot and leg tapped ninety-to-nothing, "I did but now, you tell me Cole, what else was I supposed to do when my daughter was wearing the biggest smile I've ever seen, huh? You tell me what was I supposed to do?" Minta clarified.

Moving to sit next to Minta, Cole took Minta's hand, "But doesn't a smile means she's happy? Isn't that what you want, isn't that what we all want for her?" Cole said.

Pounding her fist on top of Cole's hand, "What I want...what I want is for my daughter not to make the same mistakes I did." Minta asserted.

Releasing Minta's hand, "Mistake? Are you saying marrying my father was a mistake?" Cole asserted.

Minta's tingling skin caused her to fan herself, "Of course not Cole. Marrying your father was a blessing after what I'd gone through." Minta declared.

"Why do I get the feeling you're about to tell me something I don't know about you." Cole said.

Inhaling short, fast breaths, "Because you're right, I am." Minta acknowledged.

Bracing himself for Minta's pending revelation, Cole sat back on the sofa with open palms against the seat cushions.

Pacing about the guest bedroom floor, Minta opened with, "You know I didn't grow up with a father."

"Right." Cole affirmed.

"Well son, what you don't know is that, when the first man that paid me some attention came along...I married him." Minta disclosed.

Standing straight up from the sofa, "What?" Cole shouted.

Rushing over to Cole, "Calm down, here, sit down with me, yes, I was a young bride and it was the worst decision of my life." Minta made known.

Trying to process the words spoken by his mother, Cole's thoughts began to freeze as he wanted to keep from thinking or saying the wrong thing.

"He was charming and charismatic, just like Carson. His smile melted me like butter. He fed off of other people's energy which made him highly energetic and quite attractive. He instinctively knew how to make people feel special and at ease around him." Minta said reflecting.

"Man, I don't even know who he is and I'm already intrigued by him...go on. And uh, what's his name?" Cole replied.

"His name isn't important. What is important is that people like him have the ability to use their charming powers for both good and evil, sometimes they don't even know the difference." Minta said with a heavy sigh.

Shaking his head with his hand in the air, "What is that supposed to mean?" Cole said.

Clothed in an oversized, satin house dress Minta stood again and began to pace, "Son, this type of person can be very dangerous. The man he was to me while he courted me was much different than who he was when we married. I thank the good Lord every day I had the good sense to get out of there before he completely sucked the life out of me." Minta replied.

Dry washing his hands, Cole asked, "How long were you two married?"

Walking away to look out of the window, seeing Carson and Scarlett pull up at the house together, "We didn't make even make a year son. Every single time I look at Scarlett and Carson together, I feel like I'm looking at my younger self and the pending gloom and doom that lies ahead." Minta expressed.

"Wow, that's some deep stuff right there mom. That's some heavy revelation you just shared. But you know what, maybe Carson and Scarlett won't have to have gloom and doom, maybe and just maybe, their story will turn out differently. I mean, it's not like Carson is the first man that Scarlett has ever dated. Trust me, you can take this to dad's bank and cash it, Scarlett's had and still has options. Her story isn't exactly like yours and to be honest, you sometimes have a tendency to try and make things be about you. Now, I'm sorry that happened to you but I want to see you put all that aside and try to be happy." Cole explained.

"Maybe is a big word and maybe you're right; I just pray it does work out. However, you know what happens when a mama bear feels like her cubs are being threatened?" Minta said.

Backing up in self-defense, Cole jokingly said, "Oh no, not the mama bear; you feel like you want to attack? Please tell me you remember that show, *When Animals Attack*? I can see it now, you could be the star of a new show, *When Mama Bear Attacks*, what do you think?"

"If you don't stop making fun of me; I just might attack you." Minta said smiling. "Cole, I'm trying to settle down but I can't lie; I feel like attacking and listen, I can't be held liable for what might happen." Minta replied.

Placing his hands upon his mother's shoulders, "Whoa now, take it easy Mama Bear, everything is going to be fine. Man oh man, if you're acting like this with Scarlett getting married; I can only imagine how you're going to act when it's my turn." Cole said.

With a slow shake of her head, "Son, you have no idea." Minta said smiling as she and Cole hugged.

"Okay. Whatever that means, now I'm scared. But no, listen, you really need to calm down and enjoy this time. Scarlett is a grown woman, trust me, she can handle herself. Most of all, she's happy, let's just be happy for her." Cole suggested.

Chapter 8

"Can someone help me; I'm trying to find the most beautiful girl in the world." Carson shouts looking directly at Scarlett as he stood in the spacious entryway.

Seated alone in the Montgomery's dining room looking over the wedding program, "It all depends on who's doing the looking." Scarlett said joking.

Snapping a single rose from the freshly cut flowers that anchored the dining room table, Carson leaned in to kiss Scarlett on the cheek, "I'm doing the looking and boy have I found my good thing. You're looking beautiful this morning...as always, my dear." Carson said.

Looking up from the programs, "Ahh, thank you honey, you're not looking half bad yourself there handsome. Hey listen, I'm having so much fun, the banquet last night was amazing and don't let me get started on the golf tournament. You know that good old-fashioned butt-whipping Team Watson put on the Montgomery's, you remember, right honey?" Scarlett laughed.

Burying his head in his hand, "I'd soon like to forget." Carson said.

"Everything has been so perfect, you're perfect, I know our wedding is going to be perfect, and I'm so excited about the concert tonight." Scarlett exclaimed. "Oh, and I heard I need to thank you." Scarlett said smiling.

Shifting his eyes around, pretending to be clueless, "Thank me for what?" Carson asked smiling.

Walking over to Carson, Scarlett leaned in close and said, "I need to thank you for surprising me with getting Sherry here early. I don't know how you pulled it off without me finding out but you did. I can only imagine what other surprises you have up your sleeve Mister."

Leaning in for a kiss, "You will never need to thank me for loving you." Carson said in a whisper.

Pulling Carson closer, staring deeply into his eyes, "I love you, Carson Montgomery." Scarlett said softly.

"And I love you more baby. I'm glad you're pleased with how well everything's been going and seeing your smiling face makes me want to do everything in my power to keep you smiling." Carson admitted.

"Carson, just being with you makes me happy." Scarlett said kissing Carson.

"Yes, and I can't wait to BE with you...if you know what I mean?" Carson said returning Scarlett's kiss and caressing her body.

"Down boy, there will be plenty enough time for that and we only have a few more days to wait before we get married." Scarlett said stepping away.

"Yeah about that, there's something I need to talk to you about before we get married." Carson announced.

"Why does it sound like you're getting all serious on me, what's going on, what do you need to talk to me about?" Scarlett asked.

"Here, sit down with me. You know how I feel about you, I love you and I plan on spending the rest of my life with you." Carson explained.

Sitting down Scarlett's skin bunched around her eyes as she thought to herself speculating, "*Oh Lord, why does he sound so serious, is he thinking of calling off the wedding?*"

"It sounds like you left out a but and I don't like the way this sounds. Are you getting cold feet, are you having second thoughts? Tell me now Carson because if so, I'm out. I don't want to get married if you aren't sure." Scarlett shouted.

Waving his hands in front of Scarlett, "Calm down woman, it's nothing like that at all...geesh. Listen to me, of course I want to marry you. There are just some matters we need to address before we can say, I do. More specifically, legal matters." Carson clarified.

Settling back down, "Matters, legal matters, like what? We already have the marriage license and we'll get that signed on Saturday." Scarlett said.

Exhaling deeply, "Hmm, more than the license babe, for one, we need to go by and take a look at our new house that we'll be moving into and uh, I'm talking more like the Pre-Nuptial Agreement." Carson said.

Standing up from the table, "A prenup, you want me to sign a prenup before we can even say, I do, well guess what, hear me when I say, I don't." Scarlett shouted.

"Sweetie, c'mon, you're not being reasonable here." Carson said trying to be calm.

Pacing around the dining room, "Oh, I'm not being reasonable now. Are you serious? How reasonable is it for you to even ask me to do this? I don't understand how you want me to go look at the house we plan to move in but in the same breath ask me to sign a prenuptial agreement. Carson, do you not see you're divorcing me before we even get married? Oh, my, goodness, I don't even believe you right now." Scarlett said tapping the floor with her heeled sandals.

Walking towards Scarlett, "Now that's just not true and it is reasonable sweetheart because the reality is, we can't get married without one." Carson made clear.

Flinching her head back slightly, "Um, run that by me again, what did you just say?" Scarlett asked.

"Sweetheart...Scarlett, my love, what I said was, we will not be permitted to get married until we have a signed agreement." Carson replied.

Rubbing at her temples, Scarlett blared out, "Carson, I'm so confused by you right now. On one hand, you're promising me forever and on the other hand you're offering me a prenuptial agreement to sign just IN CASE we don't make it? Can you see how I might be having a hard time making sense out of all this? Not to mention, why am I just now hearing about this?"

Reaching for Scarlett's hand, "Listen, I know this topic isn't romantic, nothing about it is but the truth of the matter is, it's necessary. Scarlett, whether you realize it or not, marriage is yes, a spiritual and sacred act but it is also a legal one. That marriage license you talked about, legally makes us married, this agreement I'm talking about protects us both within our marriage." Carson articulated.

Dropping her hand from Carson's and walking away, "I guess I don't understand why we need protection? Carson, are you trying to back out, is this your way of backing out of marrying me? I said it before and I'll say it again, if you're unsure, let me know now; I'm not playing with you. I thought you were committed to me...to us?" Scarlett said near tears.

"Baby, baby, you're seeing this all wrong. I'm not trying to back out; I'm all in but we can't move forward and get married without a signed agreement. The church won't allow it." Carson said.

Tilting her head to the side with pursed lips, "The church? What does the church have to do with us and our marriage?" Scarlett asked.

Running his hands through his curly locks, "Um Scarlett, Scarlett, you do realize who you're marrying and what you're marrying into, right? You and I are the future of this ministry. Me and you, we're going all the way baby and the church has a stake in that." Carson said.

Slow streams of tears dropped from Scarlett's face, "What I realize is that I met and fell in love with a man named Carson who said he loved me too and wanted to get married. What I didn't realize was that would require me to sign a document that would set me up for a divorce if ever needed." Scarlett cried.

Pulling Scarlett close, "Baby, I can see you're hurt and I'm sorry about that. You're getting all caught up in the emotional and moral aspects of me asking you to do this but I promise, this is just a formality. One that has to be done in order for us to get married. Every wedding that has ever taken place within the Montgomery family has had one and not one couple has ever divorced. So, you see baby...formality." Carson said rubbing Scarlett's shoulders.

Looking up from having her head buried in Carson's chest, "Will I get a chance to look it over before it's signed?" Scarlett inquired.

"Of course, this is for both of us baby. In fact, hashing this stuff out now leaves us open to have no questions about anything going into our marriage. You need to be comfortable with everything that's in the document. Scarlett baby, you can even negotiate terms on things if you want. This is all to help us, not hurt us." Carson replied.

Sitting back down and looking over at the wedding programs again, Scarlett asked, "How long do I have before it needs to be signed?"

Checking his phone, Carson said, "Well, with all of the events planned, we need to make time to sign in the church offices with the church's counsel prior to the wedding. Therefore, whenever you feel you've had enough time, let's do it okay?"

Rolling the tension from her shoulders, "So, I guess I'll have my people call your people huh?" Scarlett said softly.

Stroking Scarlett's face, "Make no mistake about it, having to sign this document is separate from all of the love and commitment I have for you. I love you Scarlett Watson and I can't wait to make you my wife. No matter what happens in our lives; I will always love you." Carson reassured.

Chapter 9

"When are you going to start getting ready Scarlett? I believe I heard someone say your glam squad, hair and makeup will be here soon. Why aren't you getting ready for the concert?" Sherry asked.

Turning over to gaze up at the ceiling, Scarlett slowly said, "I'm not sure I'm going tonight."

Verbalizing shock, Sherry cocked her head to the side and said, "What, tell me you're joking. You are joking, right? What do you mean you're not going to a concert in your honor for your upcoming wedding?"

"Sherry, Sherry, Sherry, I just don't feel like going, is that okay? Well, even if it's not okay...I don't care. I'm not going tonight." Scarlett replied.

"Why not?" Sherry shouted.

"What part of because I don't want to go don't you understand Sherry?" Scarlett shouted bursting into tears.

Running over to sit on the bed next to Scarlett, Sherry replied, "What is going on with you girl? Are you getting cold feet, are your nerves starting to get the best of you? Talk to me Scarlett, what's going on? Do I need to call your mom?" As Sherry reached for her phone.

Sitting straight up in the bed and knocking Sherry's phone from her hands, Scarlett screamed a resounding, "No, please, whatever you do, don't call her."

Picking her phone up from the floor, "Uh thanks for knocking my phone out of my hand and if you don't want me to call or get your mom, you better speak up. What has gotten into you?" Sherry inquired.

Inching towards the edge of the bed, Scarlett said softly, pinching the inside of her hand, "Carson asked me to sign a prenup."

Upon hearing Scarlett's discontentment, Sherry lowered her head, "Are you kidding me, is that it? Carson asking you to sign a prenuptial agreement has you this out of sorts? Why?" Sherry replied.

"Why are you asking me why, why is he asking me to sign a prenup? I feel like he's setting us up to fail before we even begin. It makes me wonder, do I really know what I'm getting myself into." Scarlett confessed.

Examining her phone to make sure it still worked, Sherry scoffed, "Seriously though, you've always been such a drama queen, I thought you outgrew that but I see you haven't. You need to get your head out of the clouds, fairy tale land, or wherever you are and step into reality."

Tugging at her fluffy, terrycloth robe adorned with the Future Mrs. Montgomery embroidery,

Scarlett snapped at Sherry, "I'm not a drama queen, stop saying that."

Shaking her head with a slight laugh, "Okay drama queen, thanks for proving my point." Sherry said.

Opening her mouth to blast her cousin, Scarlett stopped short of her original thoughts and instead asked, "So, it seems you aren't having a problem with this like I am, is Glenn making you sign one?"

"The better question, my dear sweet cousin, is, am I making Glenn sign one?" Sherry said winking and giving Scarlett an easy nod. "We will not be getting married without one in place. He wasn't the happiest about it but hey, we're both lawyers, so he understands, I guess."

"What do you mean you guess, it doesn't bother you he may not be alright with it?" Scarlett asked.

Checking the time, Sherry said, "Listen, I'm not sure about you but I'm about to start getting dressed. And to answer your question, whether Glenn is 100% on board doesn't really matter to me. You know how I grew up and the way my mother has turned out. I hated seeing how she allowed men to use and abuse and I'll be, well, you know, I'll save my choice words outside of this nice Christian home. So, to me, it's a smart thing and a necessary one at that. Do you want me to take a look at it for you, do you have it with you?"

Reaching towards the night stand for the documents, Scarlett said, "I guess I hadn't looked it at from that perspective."

"I'm sure you haven't because you're all in love and not thinking clearly." Sherry said jokingly. "Seriously though, when we sat down to discuss the details, we learned so much that we needed to have straightened out before getting married and I'm so glad we did. He has thoughts about how things are supposed to go and I have mine and the prenup allowed us an opportunity to discuss important aspects of our lives and future together." Sherry added.

Blowing out a heavy breath, "I understand that and that's a good thing but I just don't understand why there has to be a prenuptial agreement standing in the way of us doing that?" Scarlett declared.

"He wants me to go and look at the house we're moving into and at the same time also harassing me to sign this agreement. Oh Jesus, I feel like I'm living in the twilight zone."

"Scarlett, listen to yourself, take your feelings and emotions out of this and look at this objectively." Sherry suggested. Looking over the documents, "Listen to me, I'm stepping out of cousin mode right now and stepping into attorney mode. Based on what I see around here and what I see in this agreement, there isn't any way this establishment, oops, I mean church is going to let you marry this guy without an agreement. You may as well get that through your head and your heart and let's make sure you have the best terms you can possibly negotiate. Right now, he's promising you the world. Get this, promises are made to be broken but a legally-binding contract is a lot harder to break. He may be offering you the world right now but trust me, this document here will assist the courts in giving it to you in the event." Sherry advised.

The knock at the door signaled to the cousins the hair and make-up team were right on time. The concert was getting closer and closer.

"Shall I let them in or shall I tell them their services are not needed this evening?" Sherry asked with a half-shrug and grin that conveyed secret knowledge.

In a monotone voice, offering little to no resistance, Scarlett answered with a small nod, "Yes, you can let them in."

Chapter 10

"Man, oh man, each night just keeps on getting better and better, don't you agree George?" Bishop asked.

With a hearty, yet genuine smile plastered across his face, "Oh yes, I have to agree with you Bishop. The artist who performed here tonight was phenomenal. His music kind of put me in the mood a little, if you know what I mean." George said rubbing elbows with Bishop.

Leaning in and talking under his breath, Bishop said, "I know exactly what you mean, I was thinking the same exact thing. You must be didn't see me whispering into Regina's ear during the concert huh?"

"What are you two over here joking about?" Regina asked as she and Minta joined their husbands.

"Oh honey, we were just admiring the view, we saw you and Minta standing over there and realized how we are two of the luckiest men around to have such beautiful wives as the two of you." Bishop replied.

Straightening out his pants, "Yep, he's right, Lord know I feel real lucky tonight." George said, kissing Minta on the cheek.

"So Minta, how'd you enjoy the concert tonight?" Bishop asked.

Before Minta could answer, she caught the eye of Michelle who was standing with Cole but staring at Carson and Scarlett.

Tapering off with her voice, Minta replied, "I, uh, I thought it was nice. Yeah, I uh, I really enjoyed myself."

Slightly touching Minta's forearm, Regina asked, "Minta, are you alright? You seem..."

"Hey look there's Carlton; I thought he'd left already; I wonder if I can get him to play maybe one or two more songs for us before he leaves." Bishop announced. Cuffing his hands around his mouth, Bishop Montgomery called out to get Carlton's attention.

Carlton Joiner, a musician friend of Regina's niece, Cherie had been the featured artist for the wedding week concert and from all accounts had done an amazing performance.

"Yes Bishop, is there something you need?" Carlton asked.

Pounding his fist over his heart, "Yeah son, you did an outstanding job tonight. We were just talking about it and wondering if you'd mind performing another little set for us, right here, maybe another song or two?" Bishop asked.

Feeling his ears turn crimson red, Carlton blushed at his requested encore, thinking to himself, *"With the check I just got from Wondrous Work; I'll perform another concert if they want me too."* Smiling at the thoughts in his heads and the zeros on his check, he graciously accepted and said, "I'd love to Bishop, just let me get my horn."

Stepping up and making a grand announcement, "Hey everyone, let's please gather around. Where's Scarlett and Carson, I especially want them in here to hear this. Carlton is going to bless us again; can someone please go and find Carson and Scarlett before Carlton comes back." Bishop announced.

Carson and Scarlett were together, out on the terrace but noticeably not the loving couple they usually were seen as. Scarlett was allowing the full weight of the prenuptial agreement to adorn her like the designer dress she was wearing. While she was trying to make sense of it and come to grips with it, undeniably, she was still struggling.

"Honey, you're a million miles away. Why won't you look at me? Kiss me." Carson demanded.

Stepping away, Scarlett retorted a sharp, "No, I don't want to kiss you right now."

"Scarlett?!" Carson replied.

Walking over towards the railing, Scarlett scanned the night sky, "I'm sorry Carson, I just...you know I should have followed my first mind and not come tonight, like I originally planned." Scarlett admitted.

Doing a double-take, "Not come tonight? In what world would you have thought that would've been alright? You're about to become a Montgomery, you can't just not come to events put on by Wondrous Works." Carson made clear.

The night air began to chill Scarlett as the breeze brushed against her bare shoulders.

Turning away with folded arms across her body, "Well, I'm not one yet. As of right now, I'm still a Watson and I can do whatever I want." Scarlett explained walking away.

Running behind Scarlett, "Hold up, where are you going? Are you still upset about the prenup, is this why you're acting this way, being all distant?" Carson inquired.

"It's a little chilly out here, I'm ready to go." Scarlett replied.

The cool night's breeze was Scarlett's excuse to leave her fiancé to chill alone.

Peeping out the door, Cole stuck his head out and said, "Oh there you two are, hey Bishop Montgomery would like for you two to come inside."

In unison, both Scarlett and Carson said, "For what?"

Smiling, Cole simply said, "Ahh, you guys are already starting to sound alike. Come in and find out."

Clapping his hands, Bishop announced, "Right on time, the happy couple is here as Carlton is coming back inside. Let's give Carlton a hand as he blesses us again."

Chapter 11

"So, how'd you enjoy the concert tonight?" Cole asked.

Michelle's eyes smoldered with intensity as her eyes burned into Cole's princely looking face, "I loved every minute of the concert. Especially every time I caught you looking over at me."

Striving to be charming, Cole smiled and said, "Well, let's just say, my eyes know where to find the most beautiful woman is in a room."

Laughing gently and tossing her head back, Michelle slipped in subtle or not so subtle question about Scarlett, "More beautiful than your sister?"

Leaning back slightly, Cole shrugged his shoulders, "Scarlett? Man, I told you before, my sister is gorgeous but I mean, I don't really look at her like that, so let me clarify, my eyes know how to find the most beautiful women in the room that I'm not related to. How's that?" Cole cleared up.

"I think I understand better now." Michelle said, leaning into Cole for a kiss.

"Well, I definitely understand this and I'd like to understand a lot more." Cole replied, returning a kiss to Michelle.

"It all depends on what you're trying to understand." Michelle whispered into Cole's ear with a flicker of her tongue.

"Based on what you just did with your tongue, I think you have an idea." Cole said, pulling Michelle closer.

With her hands stroking every inch of Cole, Michelle whispered in between kisses, "I think I do, I just need you to help me understand one thing first."

"I think we should take this to somewhere more private first." Cole suggested.

Angling her body into Cole's, Michelle offered, "Oh, we'll get to that, we can go where ever you want to go babe. I just want to know one last thing."

Consumed by Michelle's forward flirtation, Cole submitted, "What do you want to know baby; I'll tell you anything you want to know."

Out of a true fascination and desire to know, Michelle continued to kiss on Cole and asked, "How did Carson and Scarlett meet?"

Feeling energized from Michelle's inappropriate touches, Cole replied, "We can talk about all of that later, trust me, right now, I am not thinking about Carson or Scarlett. There are other matters at hand at the moment. In fact, I like what your hands are doing right now. Come on let's get out of here."

Equally as caught up in the frenzy she'd created, Michelle was ready and willing to go with Cole but was determined to continue the conversations going about the happy couple.

"Let's go but you still will tell me about Scarlett and Carson, right?" Michelle asked.

Breaking for a second, Cole stopped and asked, "Seriously, why is this so important to you? Why are you so concerned about my sister and her fiancé?"

Recognizing Cole's changing demeanor, Michelle pulled him closer and said, "I'm not that concerned babe, but you know, she's going to be the first lady of this church one day and I'm curious about their love story, that's all. You can understand that right?"

Cole's eyes followed Michelle as she reached to grab her keys.

"I see we're back to understanding some things huh? Are you grabbing your keys because we're about to finally come to an understanding?" Cole replied.

Touching her mouth, drawing attention to her lips, Michelle kissed Cole long, hard and deep and said, "I think you understand full well as to what's about to happen. Let's go."

Chapter 12

"We're here." Carson exclaimed pulling up in his two-seater luxury sports car.

Using sarcasm, Scarlett opened her car door saying, "Hooray."

"Don't be so enthused." Carson retorted, jingling the keys to open the door to their new home.

Walking inside the home, Scarlett's chest filled with pride but she did all she could to keep her inside feelings from showing outward.

Closing the door behind him, Carson fell against the custom-crafted door, letting out a pent-up breath of air saying, "Home sweet home."

Rolling her chestnut brown eyes, Scarlett waved off Carson with a simple, "Whatever."

Smiling like a Cheshire cat, Carson grabbed Scarlett by the hand and ran through the house asking constantly, "So do you like it?"

Since they'd announced their engagement, Scarlett and Carson had been designing and building their dream home, one of the many wedding gifts from the Montgomery family.

Trying to remain subdued, Scarlett smiled softly.

"Welcome to our humble abode my love. Here is where we will live together, have children together, grow old together, you name it and we're doing it all here." Carson said pulling Scarlett close to him.

"Are you sure about that?" Scarlett asked.

"Of course I'm sure, what type of question is that? Oh please Scarlett, for heaven's sake, tell me you're not still upset over the prenuptial thing?" Carson asked.

Pulling away and covertly looking around the home, Scarlett said, "You just don't seem to get it. I need you to attend to my prenuptial needs and understand where I'm coming from, not hassle me about a prenuptial agreement Carson."

Bringing Scarlett back into him, Carson smiled and said, "If you want to talk about needs; I have some that need to be addressed as well. We can go ahead and christen each and every room in this house if you want."

Scarlett's dismissive laughter, signaled to Carson, she wasn't in agreement.

"I'm going to say this to you one more time. It's not that I don't get where you're coming from, the issue is, if we are to be married, there's no way around not signing the agreement, it's that simple. If you don't sign it, we won't be able to get married. Now, I'm not going to force you to do something you don't want to do. Scarlett, if you don't want to sign it, I can respect that." Carson confessed.

"But we can't get married without my signature?" Scarlett asked.

"Unfortunately, sweetheart, we cannot. But I want you to stop focusing on the negative aspects of it and realize and know that I love you and I'm in this for the long-haul Scarlett." Carson said affirming Scarlett.

Leaning in to Carson, Scarlett whispered, "I'm going to hold you to that, Mr. Long Haul."

"And I wouldn't expect anything less." Carson replied.

Standing at the top of their stairwell, looking over their new home, their future haven, Carson and Scarlett embraced and shared an impassioned kiss of reconciliation, wrapped up in their own private world.

Chapter 13

"Good morning sweetheart, you're looking beautiful this morning...as always. How are you sweetie? Did you enjoy the concert last night Scarlett, did you guys have fun?" Regina asked.

"Good morning. I'm fine Re...I mean, Mama Montgomery. I'm alright and yes, I enjoyed the concert, how about you?" Scarlett replied.

Looking over at Scarlett, "If you say you're fine, I'll take your word for it but sweetheart, you don't seem like yourself this morning. What's going on, I hope you know you can talk to me Scarlett." Regina explained.

Mustering up a weak smile, Scarlett replied, "I'm fine."

"Okay, alright, we'll go with that. Now how about that concert, huh? Carlton is just too good; I don't know about you but I had a wonderful time last night. Are you excited about the tour at the vineyards today, sweetheart?" Regina said.

Trying to perk up a little, Scarlett smiled and said, "Yes, I am. I think I'm most looking forward to the grape stomp, I'm thinking that's going to be hilarious. What do you think?"

"I couldn't agree more, I love going out there, whenever we do one, it's the highlight of the day. The smell of ripening fruit, of the grapes, takes me back to when I was a little girl. I just love the iron gates and topiaries they have and oh good God, the beautiful artwork and décor in their sampling area is gorgeous. Can't you tell, I just love it, I'm looking forward to it as well dear. In fact, I'm looking forward to enjoying many other events with you Scarlett as a member of our family. In fact, this is why I wanted you to meet me here this morning, to discuss an important detail to you being a part of this family and our ministry." Regina said.

The whirring fan from Regina's laptop signaled she'd been busily working on things prior to Scarlett's arrival.

Exhaling an enormous sigh, Scarlett replied, "Okay, what do you have to discuss with me?"

Examining Scarlett's behavior and body language, Regina thought to herself, "*I hope all of this doesn't scare the poor child away, she looks overwhelmed.*"

Reaching into her bag, Regina pulled out a stack of indigo blue folders and said, "Well, with the wedding only days away, I need for you to select an armor bearer. Now, I've already pre-screened three young ladies who I believe will work well in this capacity and serve you well. All you need to do is look these over and choose one."

Receiving the folders from Regina, Scarlett let out another sigh saying, "Really...do I have to do this now, I think I'd like for my mother to be here to help me with this."

Sitting back in her high-back chair, Regina said, "You know, speaking of your mother, is she alright? She's been quite distant since you all got here and to be honest, it has me concerned. Not to mention, you now have me a little concerned as well honey."

Shrugging her shoulders, "You know, I guess I hadn't really noticed or have been too busy to pay attention." Scarlett replied.

Standing up from the chair with her hands thrown in the air, "Am I the only one around here noticing how off Minta seems to be? I think it's quite obvious something is bothering her." Regina scoffed.

"She may be feeling what my dad is, it's a bittersweet moment for them I guess, having their first born being married off." Scarlett tried to reason.

Walking around the dining room, Regina quieted down and said, "You're probably right and it's not appropriate for me to talk about your mother, forgive me, sweetheart. What I want to concentrate on is you and what's in these folders; I need for you to focus on this missy."

Scanning folder one, "Katrina Marks, she looks nice." Opening the second folder, "Who do we have behind door number two...Miss Jerris Ford, whoa she's gorgeous." Closing folder two quickly, Scarlett opened the final folder. "And last but not least, let's see who we have here. Miss Rebekkah Hudson, oh wow, she's pretty too. Can I ask why you've brought me all of these gorgeous women? They may outshine

me and leave me in the background." Scarlett said
laughing.

Patting Scarlett's shoulders on the way back to
her seat, "Nonsense. Scarlett, honey, these women
have nothing on you. You my dear are the chosen
one, not them, and don't you ever forget that." Regina
said sharply.

With a great deal of respect in her eyes, Scarlett
looked at her future mother-in-law and said, "I need
some help here, how'd you choose yours?"

An equal amount of respect and adoration
poured from Regina as she responded, "Listen dear,
the same thing I'm doing with you right now is the
same thing Mother Montgomery did with me and I'm
going to tell you what she said to me. Trust your
gut. Who seems to be sticking out to you? Each one
knows the sensitive nature of this part of ministry and
have assured me they are up for the job. It's just up to
you and who you feel most comfortable with."

"Okay but let me ask you this. Do I have to
have one? Is this even necessary and do I need one
now, can I please grow into some of this stuff?"
Scarlett asked.

Pouring another cup of herbal tea from her
perfectly squared and perfectly spaced out tea setting,
Regina looked over at Scarlett, "Honey, you know how
this works. I guess you don't need one but each of us
are assigned someone to assist us and I think the
sooner you get on board with how this ministry
operates, the better off you'll be. When you agreed to
marry Carson, you agreed to be on board with

everything that comes with marrying him." Regina replied.

Rubbing her hands through her hair, Scarlett took a pause and said, "Yeah, I guess you're right, I need to get on board with all that comes with marrying Carson."

Peering over the tea cup, Regina said, "Including signing the prenup?"

Looking down, unable to meet Regina's eyes, "You know about that?" Scarlett asked.

"Sweetheart, there isn't much that goes on around here that I don't know about. Carson came and talked to me about it. I hope you weren't too upset with him for asking you to sign. He was only doing as he's been instructed, it's all part of the process. He feels terrible that he may have hurt your feelings. And if you did get upset, I can understand because I was upset too." Regina admitted.

Through bulging eyes, Scarlett replied, "You were? So, I'm not crazy for feeling the way I do?"

Laughing a little before taking a sip of tea, Regina said, "No, you aren't crazy and yes, Scarlett, I can relate to how you're feeling. You actually remind me of my younger self. Trust me, I know this can all be quite overwhelming but I want you to know that I'm here for you with anything you might ever need, my daughter."

Reaching in for a hug, Scarlett smiled and said, "I really appreciate you saying that Mama Montgomery."

"I heard you went by and looked at the house earlier, what'd you think?" Regina inquired.

Scarlett's eyes brightened, "I love it, it's coming along much better than I could have imagined. I have to say, I think I was starting to get a little overwhelmed with everything but as soon as I walked in there, I felt at peace, at home."

"That's wonderful to hear sweetheart, that's how your home should feel. If I can offer anything to you right now is to just take one thing at a time, okay. And the first thing being, needs to be what's behind these folders. Why don't you look through them again?" Regina suggested.

Sorting through and studying the folders more closely this time, Scarlett's fingers slid over the smooth sheets of paper, the profiles of three women as she contemplated each folder to see if her gut signaled anyone in particular.

"I can tell someone is standing out to you, am I right? Which one is it dear heart?" Regina asked.

Still examining the folders, Scarlett took in a breath and said, "Yes, you're right. So, outside of this folder, what else can you tell me about Miss Rebekkah Marie Hudson."

Chapter 14

"The wedding bottles turned out nicely huh?" Scarlett asked inspecting the wedding wine bottles from the vineyard.

Inside the Montgomery's wine cellar, Scarlett pulled out one of the engraved wine bottles that wore the details of her pending marriage. The boxes had been delivered to the home from the vineyard.

"Uh-huh." Minta replied steadily inspecting and not looking at Scarlett.

In an effort to get her mother to open up, Scarlett said, "Wasn't the grape stomp hilarious? I couldn't stop laughing. But oh, wait a minute, that lunch at The Bolt was amazing. My favorite dish was that buttery crab meat caught directly from the Pacific Ocean and their wine has the perfect amount of crisp notes. I really think these are great favors for the wedding, don't you think so? I'm in love with the labels they created for us."

"Uh-huh." Minta replied.

Moving about the cellar, studying her mother, Scarlett stood near the marble-topped tasting table to observe Minta's response.

"Carson and I went by the house, it's turning out just as we planned. It should be ready by the time we get back from our honeymoon. You should come by and see it, what do you say?" Scarlett asked.

"Uh-huh, yeah that's nice." Minta said.

"Uh-huh, uh-huh, is that what you're going to say all day? Besides, what kind of answer is that?" Scarlett asked.

"The one I just gave." Minta said.

Raising her voice, Scarlett yelled, "What is up with you? Where is all of this attitude coming from? You know what, Mama Montgomery was right."

Finally looking at Scarlett, Minta sat down one of the wine bottles and asked, "What do you mean she was right? You already talking to her about me behind my back girl?"

Crossing her arms over her chest, Scarlett replied, "I'm not a girl and I wasn't talking about you behind your back. She's noticed you've been acting weird and asked me about it. I told her I hadn't noticed but now with you acting like this, it looks like she was right to ask."

"I beg to differ. If Regina wants to know something about me, she can come to me...woman to woman, mother to mother." Minta said mumbling and grumbling.

Shaking her head, "What has gotten into you?" Scarlett asked.

Slamming boxes from one side to the other, Minta continued to rant, "I don't know who she thinks she is questioning me. When she finds herself in my shoes, she won't have to question anything about me."

"I'm afraid to even ask but what is that supposed to mean?" Scarlett said.

Stopping for a moment, "Scarlett, let me ask you one thing. Are you sure about marrying Carson?" Minta asked.

Shouting towards her mother, Scarlett replied, "Of course, I am...I love him."

Throwing her hands in the air, Minta yelled and said, "Oh come on Scarlett, let's be real, do you love him or do you love all of this?"

"You take that back." Scarlett shouted.

"No, I will not. Someone needs to talk some sense into you; wake up Scarlett, you need to get your head out of the clouds and see what's happening right in front of you. I see too many red flags with that boy and red flags are God's warning signs for what's to come. He's not right for you Scarlett, if you go through with this, it will not end the way you think." Minta exclaimed.

Slamming her hand to the table, "But you're the only one who seems to see them mother. Don't you think by now I would have seen at least one...I haven't. I believe Carson when he says he loves me and that I'm the only woman for him." Scarlett shrieked.

"Well you're more foolish than I thought to believe in that fool. Ain't nothing about Carson Montgomery that says to me, he's ready to settle down to one woman. These people don't care about you, they are using you and when they get done with you, I'll be the one you come running back to." Minta shouted.

In a weakened voice and a bowed head, Scarlett cried saying, "It's nice to know I have such a supportive mother who speaks so highly of me. I mean, I don't know what you want from me. I've done everything you've expected of me. I went to college like you wanted; I even went to the college you wanted me to go to."

"And yes, what about that. You went to college and the day of your graduation, because Jo Blow, Carson proposed with his big shiny ring, you ditched your job offer to say yes to him. That was not the plan your father and I had for you Scarlett." Minta bellowed.

The mother/daughter duo continued to quarrel, trading jabs and insults that led to rivers of tears.

"Well, I don't need you to plan my life for me anymore. You act like you're the only one who can pray...you're not. I prayed for the right man to come for me and along came Carson and I believe he's the one." Scarlett screamed.

"Just because you prayed for a man doesn't mean God sent Carson. I'm telling you Scarlett, you're making a mistake and it's better for you to respond

now and get out before you have to suffer later."
Minta replied.

"Well it's a good thing I don't plan on suffering
and if I make a mistake, it's my mistake to make...not
yours." Scarlett scoffed.

Taking a step back, Minta looked at her
daughter and yelled out, "Oh so you think you can talk
to me like that now that you have your precious Mama
Montgomery? Well, you listen to me, you'll never
know until you have a child of your own how I feel
right now. Can't you see how my heart is breaking
right now over this Scarlett?"

Laughing and clapping her hands together,
Scarlett said, "Oh how I love how you always seem to
make things be about you. Bravo, mother, bravo."

Packing up her belongings, Minta exploded,
"Oh, you think I'm performing, well watch out
because I'm about to give you a Tony award winning
one. You're my child and I love you but I can't stand
around and watch you throw your life away on
someone who doesn't deserve it."

"Wait, what are you saying?" Scarlett shouted.

Grabbing her bag from the vineyards, in a
dramatic voice, "I can see against my sound counsel
you are determined to marry Carson and I can't be a
part of that so I'll be leaving in the morning and going
back home. I love you baby but I can't do this, I won't
do this." Minta replied.

Accidently dropping a full wine bottle and feeling a mixed spray of glass and wine, Scarlett dropped to the stoned flooring, crying and begging for her mother to stay, calling out for Minta.

With a quick glance back at her broken daughter, Minta whispered, "Good-bye Scarlett," exiting the mahogany entryway.

Chapter 15

"It's been pretty quiet around here since the grape stomp yesterday, why do you think that is?" Sherry asked.

Scarlett had not heard anything from her mother since their explosive argument. Her wandering attention had her thinking about other things while Sherry talked, which caused Scarlett to miss her question.

"Why is Sherry looking at me like that – did I miss something?" Scarlett wondered.

Scarlett could see Sherry's lips moving but the pounding thoughts in her head, thoughts of being in a tug-of-war with her mother and her fiancé' bounced around her head with such fervency, it drowned out the words being asked by her cousin.

"Okay, you didn't answer the first question so let me ask you this, are you excited about the comedy show tonight?" Sherry asked leaning in closer to Scarlett.

Trying her best to respond to Sherry, Scarlett was able to squeeze out a, "Huh?"

Sighing heavily with exaggeration, Sherry offered once again, "I've said a lot but my last question was, are you excited about the comedy show tonight? What's up with you, you seem like you're a million miles away."

Physically, Scarlett was lying in her bed for the week but mentally, she was far away. Starting to feel trapped by all of her new responsibilities paired with the displeasure shown by her mother, all Scarlett could say was a meek, "I guess."

Sitting up from under the covers, Sherry said, "What do you mean you guess? Scarlett, all of this stuff is being done for you and your wedding. This family has planned all of these elaborate events that have been nothing short of amazing and all you can say is, I guess? Here I thought Glenn and I were spending a pretty penny on our wedding but this here, literally takes the cake."

"Sherry, of course all of this is nice but...between me and you, it's getting to be a bit too much, all of it, everything is starting to get to me and I'm not sure how much more I can take." Scarlett confessed.

"Are you still upset about the fight you had with your mom? I mean, do you really think Auntie Minta is going to leave, I certainly don't. She has too much pride for that." Sherry scoffed.

Checking her phone, Scarlett smiled but hid it from Sherry, or at least tried to.

"I see you smiling over there, is that Carson saying good morning, I just got mine from Glenn." Sherry said grinning.

With a deliberate desire to avoid Sherry's question, Scarlett answered one of her others, "You asked about the comedy show earlier and yes, I'm excited about it. You know, sometimes you have to laugh to keep from crying. I think it'll be fun."

Stretching with an extended yawn, Sherry hopped out of bed, "Well that's good, I think I'm going to skip out on the comedy show, I have a few things I need to get done." Sherry said.

"What kinds of things?" Scarlett inquired.

Shaking her head, Sherry laughed and said, "You've always been a Nosey Rosie. For one, I have some work I need to do and if you must know, I have some final details to go over for Saturday night."

"Saturday night?" Scarlett replied.

"Yes, Saturday night lil Miss Rosie...some of the bridal party and I are taking you out for one last hoorah before you become Mrs. First Lady Montgomery." Sherry could barely contain her laughter as she uttered Scarlett's new last name and position. "Now that right there, calling you that, that's enough comedy all by itself."

"I can tell you find all of this amusing but I hope you aren't planning something with strippers and a whole bunch of craziness, I'm not sure the church would approve." Scarlett replied.

"Remember this, you are marrying the church, I'm not so whatever I plan is my business and not the church's." Sherry declared.

Chapter 16

Inside one of the performing arts theaters at Wondrous Works, the guests were arriving to be entertained by three of the most popular Christian comedians in the country.

The lobby was filled with people milling about trying to catch their seats before the show began.

The Montgomery family and the Watson family shared a private box, balcony seating with rows of cushioned seats. The family members filed in to their seats, well, with the exception of Minta.

Unbeknownst to the rest of the family, she was there but decided to sit elsewhere.

Three sets of flickering lights signaled the orchestra pit to get ready to start the show with an upbeat musical selection, it was show time.

Applause filled the room as the curtains opened, the custom-made scenery and props on the stage were perfect for Wedding Wednesday, the middle of the week event designed to make everyone laugh and have a great time.

Scarlett's phone rang and she quickly silenced it.

"Put your phone away baby, the show's about to start." Carson instructed.

Taking a quick glance at the message, Scarlett smiled and placed the phone in her clutch.

Prior to booking the acts, each performer was given strict instructions to structure their set and jokes around weddings and getting married.

Charles "Funny Man" Harper, the headliner was the first comedian to grace the stage. He'd be followed by "Ricky," and "Mike-Mic."

Singing and dancing his way onto the stage, Charles immediately engaged the crowd and had them laughing.

Opening up he offered, "You know that story in the bible, the parable of the three servants where a man was going on a long trip and he called his servants together and entrusted them with his money while he'd be away? Do y'all know which story I'm talking about?"

The audience agreed and chuckled, encouraging Charles to continue.

"Now that whole premise is funny all in itself if you think about it but that's not the joke I want to tell tonight, I'll save that one for another time." Charles said laughing.

Sitting on the stool brought onto the stage, Charles carried on, "Well, there was another man, he had three girlfriends and wanted to settle down but he didn't know which one to choose. So the guy took a play from the good book, he decided to go on a long trip to think about his decision but before he did, he gave each girlfriend, $5000.00 each to see how they'd spend it."

A collection of laughter and comical comments erupted from the audience.

Taking a sip of water, Charles continued to set up his joke, "When the man returned, he went to the first girlfriend to see what she'd done with the money, she said, I spent the entire amount on me, I got a complete makeover from head to toe with the money so I could look good for you because I just love you so much, what do you think? He left her and went to the second girlfriend. She reported, I spent all of the money on you, she went and gathered together all of these gifts she'd purchased. I brought them for you because I love you so much. The man, had one more girlfriend to check in with. He went to her and she said, I took the money you gave me and invested it and I've already doubled the investment. I reinvested the money because I'm investing in our future because I love you so much."

In anticipation of the punch line, the crowd speculating amongst themselves as to what happened.

"Who do y'all think he chose? Well, being the type of man he was, or let me just make it plain, being a man, he decided to marry the girlfriend with the biggest boobs." Charles joked.

The audience gushed with laughter, embarrassment, and amusement.

Throughout the rest of Charles "Funny Man" Harris' routine, he killed it, each joke, each bit he did garnered more and more laughs, it was clear and evident why he called himself a funny man.

Musical notes from down below in the orchestra hinted that the next act was up on deck.

Feeling a buzz in his jacket pocket, Carson checked his phone and saw the following message:

"Meet me in the lobby."

As he got up to leave, Carson turned to his family and whispered, "I'll be right back."

Walking down the stairwell to the lobby, the announcer was heard saying, "Next up and coming to the stage, get ready to get your laugh on with "Ricky."

Prior to walking down from the balcony seats, Carson heard Ricky saying, "A priest, a preacher, the groom, and a Rabbi walked into their favorite bar..."

Chapter 17

"Ah-ha, I see you got my message." Michelle said sneaking up behind Carson.

Clenching his jaw, through clamped together teeth, Carson begged to know, "What do you want Michelle?"

Licking her lips and running her hands across Carson's shoulders, Michelle said smiling, "Isn't it obvious; I want you and I know you want me too."

Pushing Michelle away and refuting her advances, Carson replied, "What's obvious is that you're delusional and you're starting to aggravate me."

"Aggravate you? Me, delusional? You're the delusional one if you think you're ready to get married." Michelle snapped back.

Pointing towards Michelle, "Yes, you. You are aggravating, like a gnat that won't go away and delusional to think you were anything more to me than, well, you know. For the last time, I love Scarlett, I'm in love with her and we're getting married." Carson shouted.

"Yet, when I call, you come running. Don't you ever forget; I still know how to make you come Carson." Michelle replied.

"Shut up." Carson exclaimed.

"Oh, did I hit a nerve? You know, I can hit more if you'd like me to baby." Michelle said.

In a sharp tone, Carson asked, "Are you crazy? You need help girl, get it through your thick skull; I don't want you. Do you not realize people are everywhere? My fiancé and her family could walk in here at any moment, not to mention my parents, I mean anybody could catch you. Man, this can only get ugly, I'm out of here."

Caressing her body and gyrating in front of Carson, "The more the merrier baby, maybe we can even let them watch. What do you say Carson baby?" Michelle suggested.

Walking away quickly, Carson announced, "That's it; I'm out."

"If you walk away from me; I'll tell Scarlett everything." Michelle threatened.

Stopping in his tracks, Carson walked back slowly towards Michelle facing her as if they were about to have a High Noon duel, a scorned lover's show down.

Forcing himself to remain in Michelle's presence, Carson replied, "We both know you won't do that."

Unwilling to back down, "Can't you see how hard I'm trying to keep you from making a mistake? C'mon, let's get out of here, let's go for one last time before you get married." Michelle said trying to persuade Carson.

Wrangling with Michelle to free himself from her grip, she grabs his handkerchief from his sport coat.

"That's enough Michelle, I've had it with you. From now on, when you see me, keep it moving, and don't even think about going anywhere near Scarlett." Carson demanded.

"Or what?" Michelle asked.

Overhearing the announcer broadcast a fifteen-minute intermission, Carson knew he needed to make a break and not be seen.

"Trust me, you don't want to find out." Carson replied leaving Michelle and walking down the hallway.

Realizing she had Carson's signature handkerchief in her hands, as people began to take advantage of the intermission. Michelle smiled slightly before screaming aloud. "Help, help, somebody help me. Somebody, please help me stop him. Hurry up and stop him before he gets away."

The first wave of people ignored her and continued on their way, only shaking their heads.

Using the time to contact Minta, George walked down to the lobby, hearing Michelle, he was the first to approach her, "Hey young lady, are you okay?" George asked running to assist.

"No, you need to grab him before he gets away." Michelle answered pointing in the direction Carson left in.

"I'm not sure I understand, tell me what's going on again?" George asked.

"You need to go and catch Carson." Michelle roared.

Reaching for his phone, George sent out a quick group text that read:

"Come down to the lobby now."

One by one, the family rushed down to the lobby, including Minta.

A small crowd started to gather to observe. The comedy had been happening on the inside but all of the drama was taking place outside.

"What is going on in here, what's all this commotion about?" Regina asked.

Holding Michelle's hand, "That's what I'm trying to find out now. She said something about stopping Carson." George said.

Putting on a show, Michelle turned on the hysterics, "Somebody needs to stop him, he tried to..."

Scarlett and Bishop Montgomery followed soon thereafter.

"We all got your text, what's going on dad?" Scarlett asked.

Upon seeing Scarlett, Michelle kicked up her performance into high gear.

Inconsolable and terribly upset, Michelle cried, "You need to stop Carson before he gets away. He just tried to...oh my God, I can't even say the word. He just tried to force himself on me but I pushed him off and started screaming and then he ran off." Holding up the handkerchief as evidence, Michelle continued, "See, as I was fighting for my life, he left this behind as he ran away."

In their own way, everyone standing in the room, reacted to Michelle's allegations.

Throwing a hand to her head, Regina exclaimed, "Oh dear God."

Repeating back what was said, Scarlett raises up, "Hold on a second, did I just hear Carson and attempted rape in the same sentence?"

Coming out of character, Michelle replied, "Yes, your future husband just tried to get all of this."

"This is a very serious accusation, are you sure about this young lady?" Minta asked.

"And I thought you were leaving?" Scarlett mumbled.

Pacing in short spans, Michelle shouted, "Why are you all asking me all of these questions when you should be trying to find Carson."

"Hey, everybody, what's going on, have I missed something?" Cole asked.

Looking directly at Cole, Michelle runs towards Cole, takes in a breath and says, "Hey babe, I hate to tell you this but your sister's fiancé tried to force himself on me and no one will go find him. You'll help me, won't you Cole-y?"

All of the family turns to Cole and in unison shout, "Babe? Cole-y?"

Crossing his arms, showing his closed off body posture towards Michelle, "Stop it because I'm not the one. First of all, I'm not your babe and secondly, you're lying." Cole said with a dismissive wave.

Interestingly enough, Michelle's tears dried up as she scolded the group, "Oh that's right, blame the victim. You all should be ashamed of yourselves."

Baiting Michelle, Cole shook his head while saying, "No, you should be ashamed. You are living foul Miss Michelle and I'm sorry I ever hooked up with you. It all makes sense, now I see why you were asking me so many questions about my sister and Carson. But I have you now, you see, my man Carson didn't do what you're accusing him of."

"Carson is the foul one, he tried -." Michelle squealed.

Stepping out of the restroom, Carson looked down the hall and saw his family encircled around Michelle. Unsure as to what was happening, he slowly turned the other way and left the building.

Interjecting Michelle's rant, Cole took out his phone and announced, "Oh I know who tried what; I have proof."

Trying to keep up the charade, "Proof? I don't care what kind of proof you think you have, it doesn't excuse Carson of his actions." Michelle sneered.

Having his phone cued up, Cole walked over to everyone and hit the play button on his phone. "Take a look at this everybody, if a picture is worth a thousand words, this video must be worth a million."

With all eyes on Cole's phone, Michelle slapped the phone from his hands onto the floor. "I don't know how he got whatever it was he had." Michelle shouted.

Picking up his smashed phone from the floor, Cole stood smiling, "What they didn't see in the video, I'll gladly tell. You see, you sent me a text saying to meet you in the lobby so I was coming to look for you. Imagine my surprise when I see you trying to come onto Carson. Man, he pushed you away so fast, he flat out shut you down. Dang baby, attempted rape? You could have at least come up with something more original. I mean that's like one of the oldest tricks in the book...the good book that is." Cole explained.

Shaking her head, Regina let out a heavy sigh, "My God, my God. Potiphar's wife did the same thing to Joseph and now she's doing the same to my son." Regina whispered.

"Michelle?" Bishop asked with grave concern.

Feeling trapped and backed into a corner, Michelle lashes out and points towards Minta, "I. I. I'm sorry but she made me do it."

Rising up quickly and responding in a sharper tone, "The devil is a liar, I did no such thing." Minta exclaimed.

The onlookers stood watching enjoying their refreshments ordered during the intermission.

Stepping towards Michelle in a threatening way, "First you lie to me, then you lie on my buddy, my soon to be brother-in-law, and now you're lying on my mom. Who are you? All I know is you might want to get lost and soon." Cole demanded.

Putting some space between Cole and Michelle, George stepped in to calm Cole down, "Back up son." George ordered.

In an effort to deflect the attention from herself, Michelle walks closely towards Minta, speaking loudly for everyone to hear, "Oh so you didn't pull me over to the side the other night at the reception where we hatched a plan for me to come onto Carson so we could stop the wedding from happening?" Michelle publicized.

Feeling let down but holding out hope for a different resolve, George with his pinched expression looked at Minta and mouthed, "Please tell me this isn't true."

Minta's thickening voice was almost unrecognizable as she tried to explain, "What is true is that I did confront this young lady with my suspicions about her and Carson, which she did CONFIRM. BUT, I NEVER conspired with her about accusing him of such a despicable act; I would NEVER do that."

Glaring at Michelle with eyes that appeared cold and flat, Regina stood in front of Michelle and let into her, "It's people like you who make it hard for REAL victims to speak up. You are disgusting and you should be ashamed."

Michelle, refusing to look at Regina turned to walk away but stopped to hand Carson's kerchief to Scarlett, "Good luck with your marriage." Michelle said.

Rubbing the kerchief over her fingertips, shaking her head and muttering, Scarlett walked over to her mother and simply said, "I can't believe you."

"Honey, listen to me." Minta begged.

Feeling betrayed, "No, you listen to me. And to think I was hurt you were leaving and not going to be here for my wedding. Silly me. You said you can't stand by and watch me marry Carson and that you're leaving. Well, now, I don't care whether you stay or go. In fact, it might be better if you did just pack up and leave. Regardless of your decision, you've helped me a lot with mine, given your little stunt here. You should know, whether you like it or not, I will be marrying Carson for better or worse." Scarlett replied walking away.

"Scarlett, come back sweetheart, let's sit down and talk about this, don't walk away honey." George pleaded.

Scarlett dismissed her father's pleas and continued walking away, walking past the latest engagement photo Regina had planned to reveal.

Chapter 18

Pacing the floor in the bedroom of the guest house, George hung his hands on his hips, "For the life of me, I can't begin to understand why you would do such a thing Minta, can you please explain to me what you must've been thinking? You have to make me understand this." George pleaded.

"That's my child." Minta snapped back.

Folding his arms across his chest, "Oh, is, that right? So, I guess you had her all by yourself, huh?" George mocked.

Throwing her hands in the air, rummaging through her things, "Oh whatever George. You know what I mean and hey, I didn't do anything any different from any of these other mothers out here wouldn't do. As you can see, I'm willing to do whatever it takes, even if it means...doing what I did. I was trying to protect her." Minta replied.

"But instead, you hurt her. Or don't you see that? Minta, your determination has driven you to extremes that are highly disappointing and reckless. Not only that, you've embarrassed yourself, our family, and I'm sure the Montgomery's. Did you happen to take note of all the people standing around watching what was going on?" George shouted.

Searching for a bottle of water to quench her intense thirst and dry mouth, in a flash of anger,

Minta yelled back quickly, "Do you think I care about the Montgomery's right now?"

Minta's actions were born out of the fear of losing her daughter by way of marriage but she was having a hard time articulating that. The dependence she had towards Scarlett was unhealthy and it was causing Minta to uncharacteristically act out.

Pointing his finger directly at his wife, "I don't care whether you do or not, but you better. Thanks to you, OUR daughter is now more determined to marry that boy. You've just ensured we're going to be tied to this family for a long time. Let me ask you something Minta, have you for once considered what this must be like for me?" George asked.

Stumbling and stuttering trying to find an answer, Minta was unable to find the right words.

"Exactly Minta. You've only been concerned about how you feel and no one else. Do you think I want my baby girl to be hurt by Carson? Absolutely not but it's her decision and the best thing I can do for her is to respect her decision." George declared.

Minta plopped her body on the cushy bed, her stomach had become hardened, a burning sensation filled her chest, and her breaths came faster and more coarse. "But George, you don't seem to get it. They've shut us out of everything. They are trying to take our daughter from us. I mean, they didn't ask us anything, we have had no input. There has been no consideration as to whether or not, we wanted to pay for our daughter's wedding. I mean, they aren't the only ones with money. I plan parties and events, what if I wanted to help with the details of my daughter's wedding, huh? Regina now wants my daughter to call her mama, give me a break. I'm her mama, the only one she'll ever have." Minta shouted.

Minta increased the volume and intensity of words as if she wanted Regina to hear them all the way through to the other side of the sprawling estate.

In her continuous rant, "Had I known when I took this consultation that my daughter would end up marrying this clown; I would have never taken this gig." Minta blared.

Rubbing the back of his neck, George felt a heaviness come over him, "Minta, this is silly and now you're just being mean and petty. It is what it is, you need to get a grip and stop cutting up."

Stomping around with what sounded like lead feet, Minta, blowing up at George, shrieked, "Who's side are you on George?"

Retaliating without thinking, George quickly said, "Who's side am I on, really Minta? Really?"

"I carried her in my belly for nine months, I was the one who went through the pain of delivering her and I just don't want anything bad to happen to her. You know I didn't have anybody to protect me and all I'm doing is trying to save her." Minta said obsessing and crying.

Hard for him to, George slowly walked over to comfort Minta, he was very upset with his wife's actions.

"Yes, you had her but it's time to let go. When she was born, the doctors let me cut the cord but you haven't. Minta, she's a grown woman and she deserves your respect." George declared.

Crying through her pain, "It's just so hard George; I just don't know if I can let go." Minta admitted.

"You can and you will. As a matter of fact, you're going to do more than that Minta. You will apologize to everyone and you will be at that wedding, you're not going anywhere." George stated.

Trying to interject, Minta raised her finger but George continued, "Not only will you be at the wedding but you will be happy about it. You will smile and you will not say anything out of line, do you hear me?"

In an attempt to interject again, this time, Minta raised her hand, however, George had more to say. "And another thing, if and only if you're right about Carson and he ends up breaking our baby's heart, we will be there for her. There will be no, I told you so's or anything like that Minta and I mean it. If and only if that time comes, we will be there as her parents to help her through whatever. Have I made myself clear here?"

Settling herself on the bed to begin a long answer, her husband responds for her, "Uh-uh, or a yes is all I'm looking for here. I'm not playing with you about this Minta. I've had about my fill with you. Enough is enough." George shouted.

Through clenched teeth and an aggravated snarl, Minta finally answered with a, "Yes George."

Chapter 19

"Eugene, Eugene, I told you to talk to that boy and now look. Did you talk to him at all?" Regina inquired.

Collapsing onto his leather, swivel chair, Bishop Montgomery held his head down and answered, "No honey, not yet. With everything that's been going on, I hadn't had a chance to get him alone to speak with him."

Regina's pointy finger zeroed in on her husband's face, "Then you were supposed to make time Eugene. This whole thing is getting completely out of hand."

"Regina calm down." Bishop said.

"I will not calm down Eugene. I asked you to talk to Carson and you didn't and now we have a disaster, a mess, another mess on our hands. Do we want to become the type of preachers who talk against sin for others but accept it and condone it as parents? Eugene, this situation is becoming more and more problematic and you know it. Or at least, I think you know but part of the problem is these blind spots you seem to have concerning our sons." Regina blared out.

Tapping his finger against his lips, Bishop remained silent as Regina continued to explode in Bishop's office.

"Am I talking to myself here, why aren't you talking to me?' Regina asked.

"Regina, give me a minute. I mean, I'm trying to take a second to digest everything that's happened. Now listen, the girl lied, Carson didn't do what she said he did." Bishop replied.

"She may have lied about who forced themselves on whom but the truth of the matter is she and Carson has or had something going on. Oh my Lord, I can only imagine what the Watson's must be thinking right now." Regina said.

Playing a game of what if, Bishop Montgomery wanted to understand the repercussions of the situation. "What if everyone is fine and this isn't a big deal like you're trying to make it?" Bishop asked.

"And what if they are freaking out and planning to pack up and leave, did you not hear Scarlett say her mother was planning to leave before the wedding?" Regina shouted.

Standing up from his seat and adjusting his clothes, "Oh and about her mother, can you believe what she did?" Bishop replied.

"While I'm madder than a one-legged woman at IHop at Minta for what she did; I can't say I blame her. She confronted what we wouldn't Eugene. Her daughter is getting ready to marry our son and she obviously has concerns. I told you from the moment she arrived that something was off with her." Regina explained.

Glancing at his watch, Bishop didn't immediately respond.

"Am I boring you? Do you have somewhere else you need to be right now?" Regina instigated.

Checking the time once again, Bishop responded to his wife's questions, "Regina, please calm down with all of that. I was checking the time because you know mother is due back later tonight. I wanted to make sure I had enough time to make arrangements for her to get from the hanger. Is that alright with you?"

"Hmm, I wonder what she'll have to say about all of this?" Regina said with a soft smile.

"I may not tell her." Bishop confessed.

Regina was beyond fed up, the stress and strain from always having to cover up Carson's indiscretions bothered her.

"See that's your problem, you want to hide and cover up this mess. If you don't tell her, I will and another thing, if you don't talk to Carson, then I'm going to do that too. And trust me, neither one of you will like what I have to say. The wedding is in a few days, things need to be settled Eugene. Speaking of Carson, has anyone heard from him, do you know where he is right now?" Regina said.

Taking a peak at his phone, Bishop said, "I don't know where he is. I've called him and I've reached out to Godfrey to see if he knows where he is."

"And what did Godfrey say?" Regina asked.

"He said, Carson told him not to worry about supporting him this week and if he needed him, he'd call him." Bishop replied.

"This isn't good." Regina said pacing the floor.

"And I haven't heard from Carson, he isn't answering my calls or texts." Bishop added.

A knock at the door interrupted Regina and Bishop's conversation.

Upon opening the door to Bishop's office, they both heard, "I'm back, did y'all miss me while I was gone?" Mother Montgomery said smiling.

Walking over to help Mother Montgomery inside, Bishop asked, "Mother, what are you doing here? You weren't supposed to be here for another two hours or so. What happened?"

"Well hello to you too son. Nothing happened, only that I spoke with the pilot and was able to catch an earlier flight and I took it." Mother Montgomery explained.

Reaching in to greet her mother-in-law, Regina kissed Mother Montgomery on the cheek and said, "Nice to have you back Mother, how was your trip?"

"Nice to see you Regina and I'm glad to be back. You know, my trip was lovely. I'm glad I had a chance to celebrate my long-time friend, Lani's birthday. When you get to be my age, our age, birthday celebrations are important and necessary. The bible says, a sweet friendship refreshes the soul, I can truly say, my soul has been refreshed." Mother Montgomery said chuckling.

"I'm glad you had a nice trip but you couldn't call us to let us know you were arriving earlier? Mother, it's late and I don't like it that you're out here alone. How'd you get here?" Bishop gasped.

"Oh Eugene, hush your fuss; I'm here aren't I? I just thank the good Lord that I made it home safely. Even though I had a good time, it was hard for me to concentrate because all I could think about is this wedding. You all know how much I love wedding week. I hate I missed Wedding Wednesday too, Lord knows, I was trying to hurry back for the comedy show. So tell me, how's wedding week been, what have I missed?" Mother Montgomery inquired.

Chapter 20

"Hey, you awake over there?" Sherry asked.

The perfect moment of the sun peeking over the horizon with its brilliant and striking colors was announcing the break of day.

"Scarlett, I know you aren't asleep and if you are, wake up, did you forget we have a spa appointment coming up?" Sherry asked.

Sitting down on the bed, Scarlett's blank features indicated to her cousin that something was wrong.

In an attempt to move Scarlett along so they wouldn't miss their appointment, Sherry announced, "This lady from the church stopped by to remind you of the spa appointment. She said something about how in the Bible times, brides made themselves ready through some sort of purification process. I don't know what all of that means but I am getting married too and I'd like to take advantage of this free full spa day style treatment the church is offering. C'mon Scarlett, let's get ready to go."

Burying herself under the covers, making herself small, Scarlett hugged herself into the fetal position, "I'm not going to the spa." Scarlett replied.

Sighing with exaggeration, "Heavens to Murgatroyd, what is it now Scarlett? First you weren't going to the concert, now you aren't going to OUR spa day, are you still tripping over the prenuptial agreement?" Sherry inquired.

"No."

"No what Scarlett?"

Staring off at nothing, Scarlett said, "No, I'm not still tripping over the agreement because I'm probably not going to sign it."

"Why not? I thought we went over this." Sherry said.

Sherry didn't know what to think after Scarlett's long and extended exhale.

"You were asleep when I got back last night so you don't know what happened, you haven't heard the latest." Scarlett said speaking in a monotone voice.

"Heard about what?" Sherry asked.

Sitting up on the bed, Scarlett looked over at her cousin, "Sherry, I really don't even have the strength right now to discuss it." Scarlett replied.

Wagging her finger in front of Scarlett's face, Sherry urged, "Oh no honey, if we're going to miss OUR spa appointment, you're going to have to come on with the come on. Spill it, what happened?"

Scarlett explained to Sherry what transpired the night before but what felt like a lifetime ago. Scarlett sensed she was stuck in a time warp, stuck between her past, present, and future and unsure how to navigate any of it.

Cracking her knuckles as if she was prepping to go into battle, Sherry shouted, "Where is she? Better yet, where is he? This right here is some bull..."

"Sherry." Scarlett yelled back.

"What? You're the one that has to pretend to be holier than thou, not me. I've been trying to be on my best behavior around these church folks but this here wedding week is making me weak. This is ridiculous. Now I see why you may not go through with it." Slinging her head back sharply, "Ugh, I could kill Carson, how could he?" Sherry exclaimed.

"Calm down Sherry." Scarlett said softly. Falling back onto the down feathered comforter, "Thing is, I haven't even cried; I don't know why I'm not upset. I don't feel hurt, betrayed, I don't feel any of the words or feelings I guess I should have in this situation. I mean, I just don't feel anything right now." Scarlett admitted.

"You're probably in shock and you might be numb from everything that's going on. Have you talked to Carson to find out his side?" Sherry asked.

Staring up at the ceiling, Scarlett answered, "No, I haven't. He's called several times and texted me but I haven't responded yet. I don't think I even know how."

With a sly looking smile, Sherry stood over Scarlett and said, "I think a hot stone massage could help you figure things out. I'll gather our things, we still have time to make it. C'mon, get up."

Slowly rising from the bed back to a seated position, Scarlett spun Carson's engagement ring around on her finger, "Gregory called me last night." Scarlett revealed.

Stopping in her tracks, Sherry, gently walked backwards towards Scarlett and declared, "Run that by me again."

"I said, I talked to Gregory last night." Scarlett made known.

"Here we go again, this here wedding week is making me more and more weak. Excuse me but why are we talking to Gregory days before walking down the aisle? Ding, dong, uh hello, the rest of your bridal party will be tomorrow, have you forgotten? I thought you were through with him? What is going on with you Scarlett?" Sherry questioned Scarlett as if she was in court on the witness stand.

If an analogy were to be used, kryptonite was to Superman as Gregory was to Scarlett.

Gregory Sanders, a young professor, Scarlett met in her last year of college, by taking one of his classes.

Their relationship started out innocently enough. After class questions turned into email conversations that turned into the exchange of personal contact information that lead into coffee shop invitations that led into private meetings.

Of course, student/teacher relationships were forbidden at the small, Christian college but certainly, married teacher/student relationships were not allowed. In a setting where future apostles, preachers, teachers, evangelists, and prophets roamed the halls of the campus, there was positively no place for adulterers and fornicators.

Yet, Scarlett knew Gregory was off-limits but his off-the-mark, mysterious nature made him immensely attractive. They tried to resist the temptation but they failed. Knowing full well, he was no good for her, she fell for him anyway and he for her.

Married to a woman with a terminal illness, he sought solace and consolation with Scarlett during their non-sanctioned, non-office hour meetings.

His office had become their hideaway from the rest of the world. They met often and each time, shared their mutual and shared attraction for one another on top of the papers he should have been grading.

The personal pictures of Gregory and his wife would oftentimes have front row seats to their decadent trysts.

Then there were times inside his office where they'd explore the true meaning of the words, "love seat," where they shared theirs.

Sometimes when they'd arrive, the normal flick of florescent lights would quickly be turned off because all they needed was the warm glow from his computer screen. The two had mastered the art of finding each other in the dark. The walls in Gregory's office absorbed the details of their relationship and held them in confidence. The walls, devoid of any real decoration, with the exception of one single motivational poster, with one word in bold, upper cased letters, that read, **BELIEVE**. Which was ironic because no one would ever believe what Gregory and Scarlett were doing.

Over the years, Minta had warned of bad boys and not bringing any home and while Gregory was no "Billy Joe Bad Boy," Scarlett could never bring him home. Growing up, Scarlett had always played by the rules, she was perfect at it but being with Gregory made her want to break every single rule there was.

Scarlett's good girl image remained intact as long as she wasn't around Gregory. Around him, being good wasn't a concern, she was only concerned with how bad of a girl she could be when she was with him. In private, her puritan persona, was exchanged for a fleshly and empowered, sensual experience.

His touch was electric, it was more than a physical one, it sometimes felt more spiritual and his fingers could burn holes into her silky, supple skin. Gregory was irresistible and the power of their attraction and connection was sometimes uncontrollable, too much for either of them to handle.

"His wife died two months ago." Scarlett whispered.

Unmoved, Sherry asked, "And? What does that have to do with you?"

"Nothing Sherry, goodness gracious, he just wanted me to know. But let me ask you, with everything going on do you not find it strange that he's coming back around?" Scarlett replied.

"Um, no I don't find it strange, sometimes that's how life works but let me ask you, now that you know, now what Scarlett? Does he even know you're getting married?" Sherry asked, matter-of-factly.

Shifting her weight on the bed, Scarlett squirmed, tilting her head, and squealed, "Um, yes and no."

Drawing in slow, steady breaths, Sherry asked, "It's a yes or no answer, so which is it? Based on how you squirmed in that bed, I pretty much know the answer. Am I right about it?"

"Dang Sherry, you're interrogating me like I stole something." Scarlett scoffed.

"Uh Scarlett, you kinda did, Scarlett the Harlot. Now, I know what you did isn't exactly first lady resume material so I won't go into all of that right now in case these good church folks have cameras on us." Sherry whispered while looking around for hidden cameras.

Sherry's search around the room appealed to Scarlett's sense of humor and she responded with a full belly laugh.

"Sherry, girl, you are crazy...Scarlett the Harlot, that was a good one. You see, that's why you shouldn't share your secrets because people always try to use them later on you." Scarlett said laughing uncontrollably.

Ending her search, Sherry sat shoulder to shoulder with Scarlett. "Alright 'Lil Miss, what's it going to be? All I'm saying is, I'm not here to judge you, I'm the last person to do that. It seems as if you have some unfinished business, just make sure you handle it." Sherry encouraged.

Lowering her head to the top of Sherry's shoulder, Scarlett whispered, "I will big Cuz, I can't thank you enough for being here to help and support me through all of this."

"That's what family is for but uh if you won't take advantage of an all-expense paid spa day...I will. Therefore, I'm going to give you some time alone and I'm going to go get pampered. My honey will be here tomorrow so I'm going to get purified, isn't that what the lady said? Whatever it is, I'll be back later." Sherry said smiling.

Drowsily, Scarlett yawned and replied, "Okay, enjoy yourself, I'm tired, I feel drained; I think I'm going to go back to sleep."

Chapter 21

"Carson? Where are you son?" Mother Montgomery asked.

Ignoring everyone else's attempts to reach out to him, Carson could never ignore his grandmother's calls. The missed calls and the unread texts were piling up in his phone but Carson didn't care. However, when Mother Montgomery called, he answered.

Calling to inquire of his whereabouts, Mother Montgomery had no idea where he was. Little did she know, he wasn't far at all. In fact, he was right in their backyard.

Mother Montgomery had a way with saying Carson's name, the drawl, she attached, she would draw it out saying it like, *Cah-sun*.

"Talk to Mother, tell me what's going on with you boy?" Mother Montgomery encouraged.

Seated high above the vegetable garden, Carson's legs dangled through the trap door of his old tree house.

"I messed up...again." Carson confessed.

"So you were messing around with that girl?" Mother confirmed.

"Yes ma'am." Carson said softly.

"Carson, what's the matter? Are you scared? Do you not want to get married?" Mother Montgomery questioned.

Feeling a burning in his heart, the culpability of his reckless abandon times one hundred was beginning to manifest itself physically. Carson's self-destructive behaviors connected with his body and he felt it. His heart was confused by the love he held for Scarlett coupled with the guilt he felt for constantly messing up.

Seated on the musty, nappy carpet Carson held his head down and said, "I don't know. I'm only scared because I don't know what Scarlett must be thinking, she won't return any of my calls. You know, I still don't know what all happened. When I came out of the bathroom and saw all of them standing there talking to Michelle, I left."

"And you haven't spoken to anyone since son? Oh Carson. Where are you, maybe you should come by the house and sort things out?" Mother Montgomery suggested.

Staring at the *Keep Out* sign barely hanging on the door, Carson let out a huge sigh. It'd been years since the Montgomery boys had been inside their beloved treehouse.

This was not a traditional treehouse, it was a prefabricated home outfitted with glass windows, decks, and slides, it just happened to be located in a tree.

In his troubled heart and mind, this rite of passage of a hideout was the place he decided to return to.

Flipping through the dated, glossy pages of his girly magazines, Carson asked, "Have you seen or spoken to Scarlett?"

"No, I haven't son. I got in last night and I've only spoken to your parents who filled me in on everything. Let me ask you something Carson, are you marrying Scarlett because Regina likes her so much or do you really love her and you want to get married?"

Carson's gritty, dry eyes from lack of sleep, welled up with water, "Yes, I love her and I want to marry her. Having my mother love her too is just gravy. I may have messed up but I'm not messed up over how I feel about Scarlett; I'm clear on that."

"Well, let me ask you this, are you sorry for what you've done and how would you feel if she did this to you?" Mother Montgomery inquired.

Crumpling on the dusty loveseat, thinking back on all of his past transgressions, muttered to himself, *"What have I done, how could I have let this happen?"* Mother Montgomery's last question hit him hard, it took what little wind he had left completely out. Taking a moment to answer, Carson responded to his grandmother by saying, "I make mistakes and I do stupid things and until now I never really cared or thought about how it affected other people but now I'm very sorry for what I've done and what this must be doing to Scarlett. The thought of her hurt and crying over some of my B.S. hurts because I don't know what I'd do if the roles were reversed."

"A broken spirit and a contrite heart, God will not despise.[1] Right now your heart is tender towards God and Scarlett, at this point, based on what you've done and the regret and remorse you have, you can allow God to mold you into the man and husband he's called you to be. And if you're feeling hurt because of what your actions have done to Scarlett, then go and tell her that. Confront this situation head on. You don't want her crying, speculating and questioning things. Go and nip this thing in the bud, handle it, you're the only person who can make this right and set things straight." Mother Montgomery admonished.

"You're right, as always, you are absolutely correct. You are the best grandmother ever; I truly appreciate your wise counsel." Carson acknowledged.

"Listen to me now, there's a lot going on, things I'm sure you're not even aware of but I'm going to be praying and my prayer is that everything works out how they're supposed to. Okay? Now, go and take care of your business son. Mother loves you." Mother Montgomery declared.

"Yes ma'am, I'll talk to you later." Carson replied.

---

[1] **Psalms 51:17**: "The sacrifices of God are a broken spirit: a broken and a contrite heart, O God, thou wilt not despise. (**KJV**)

Chapter 22

"Scarlett...baby...wake up, do you mind if we talk?" Carson whispered, kneeling down beside Scarlett's bed.

Watching her sleep made Carson smile, Scarlett looked so peaceful, he hated to wake her and break such a beautiful and serene scene but he needed to talk.

Whispering once again, "Baby, it's me, wake up." Carson said softly.

Startled and in between consciousness and unconsciousness, Scarlett yelled, "No, I don't ever want to go back there, stay with me."

Standing up and grabbing a swinging Scarlett, Carson exclaimed, "Hey, hold up girl, you having a bad dream or something, wake up."

Realizing she was no longer asleep and in a dream state, Scarlett took a moment to get her bearings together.

"Oh hey...good morning. I guess I was having a bad dream. What are you doing here Carson?" Scarlett said lying back down on the bed in the opposite direction of Carson.

Walking around the bed to face Scarlett, Carson stooped down to look her eyeball to eyeball. "Hey listen, I know you're upset but can we please talk?" Carson asked.

Scarlett's dejected sigh and blank features led Carson to believe his work was cut out for him.

"C'mon baby, get up and let's talk this through." Carson urged.

"Do your parents know you're in here? Have you seen them since last night? Scarlett asked.

"No, I snuck in...no one knows where am I. They've been calling me but I've only spoken to my grandmother, now come on, get up, I'd like to talk to you." Carson replied.

Helping Scarlett from the bed, Carson held both of her hands and led her to the sitting area within the bedroom.

"So that was some dream you were having there huh?" Carson asked trying to break the ice and feel out Scarlett.

"If he only knew what I was dreaming about, I'm glad it's stuck safe and sound, snuggling in between my ears, in my brain." Scarlett thought.

"Yeah I guess." Scarlett said, offering little.

"I've been calling and texting you." Carson said.

"I know." Scarlett replied.

The tension between the couple was more than thick, there was no way you could cut this, it would need to be sliced instead.

Recognizing in order to reach Scarlett, Carson realized he needed a different approach.

"First of all, baby...I need you to know; I never meant to hurt you. I heard about what happened and I know a thousand I'm sorry(s) aren't even enough to make up for what I've done but I at least want to start with one, I'm sorry and I pray you can forgive me." Carson said.

"Why did you leave the concert without saying anything?" Scarlett asked.

"To be honest, I panicked. I didn't know what was going on, all I knew was that whatever was happening it didn't look good from where I was standing, so I left. I needed some time to clear my head and to think...and to pray." Carson admitted.

Resting her head onto her fist, Scarlett asked, "So what's going on with this Michelle girl, why would she go through such lengths and lie on you like that and why does my mother hate you so much?"

Standing from the sofa, Carson took a thoughtful stretch, "Who knows, I've only ever been nice to your mother; I have no idea why she hates me and to think she conspired with Michelle to try and break us up. I can't believe that."

"Now wait a minute Carson, my mother wouldn't have had to conspire if there wasn't anything to conspire with." Scarlett said defending her mother.

Even after all Minta said and threatened, Scarlett still stood up for her mother.

Nodding his head in agreement, "You're right and I'm wrong. Scarlett, I may have grown up in the church and may be in line to take over the church but I've never pretended to be a saint. Honestly, you need to know, I've done some things in my past I'm not proud of but I'm ready to put all of that behind me and start a life with you." Carson acknowledged.

"Is Michelle one of those things you've done?" Scarlett asked.

Carson's face, neck, and ears felt increasingly hot, pulling at his collar, in an attempt to let in some cool air, Carson looked at Scarlett and answered her question, "Yes, but she's in my past. You, Scarlett baby are my present and in my future."

Shaking her head slightly, Scarlett replied, "Carson, I know you want to take over the church and all but maybe we aren't ready and maybe I'm not the one to help you fulfill that role in your life."

The church was within reach, getting married was one of the final requirements but hearing Scarlett's words, Carson began to feel a shakiness in his limbs.

Kneeling down beside Scarlett, Carson asked, "Why are you saying this, is it because of what happened with Michelle? Baby, I don't want her, she was just something I was passing the time with. I want you, you're the one I'm choosing to marry, not her or anyone else. You are the one, the one who will stand by my side and be the face of this ministry."

Respecting Carson's level of honesty, Scarlett loosened up somewhat. "Are you sure things are done with her? Is there anyone else who might show up and try something?" Scarlett asked.

Sitting down beside Scarlett, Carson picked up her hand and looked into her eyes. "Scarlett, I'm done with her and all the craziness. From this day forward, I promise to love and cherish you. Scarlett, baby, I've never met anyone like you, you are all I've ever wanted and needed. You make me want to be a better man, a man you deserve." Carson promised.

"Don't make any promises you can't keep." Scarlett suggested.

Holding up his pinky finger, "Well, you know the only way to make a promise official is to pinky-promise, right?" Carson said smiling.

"I don't even want to know why you know that." Scarlett said jokingly.

The two shared a laugh and Carson linked his pinky onto Scarlett's pinky as they shook on it.

"Hey listen, are we good? I want to see what you think about an idea I just got. The family barbeque is tonight but what if we skipped and hung out, just the two of us?" Carson suggested.

"Well Carson, I appreciate your honesty and I mean, technically, we aren't married yet so..."

Scarlett's pause, caused slight concern for Carson. What was she about to say?

"If we're being honest, there are somethings I've done in my past that I want to leave there...in the past." Scarlett shared. "And again, if I'm being honest, I could use a break from the wedding activities, so hanging out sounds nice."

Thinking to herself, "*I want to leave Gregory in my past but he's trying to reinsert himself back into my life but I'm not going to let that happen. I just need to let him know I'm getting married.*"

Waving his hands in the air, "Oh no, don't you dare ruin my perfect image of you. I don't want to hear anything about what or who you may have done before me; I wouldn't be able to take it. I'm going to plan something so fun for us tonight but all I want to know is, are you ready to do this thing? Are you ready to become Mrs. Carson Eugene Montgomery IV and my first lady?" Carson asked.

Holding hands on the sofa, Scarlett answered, "Yes, I'm ready and I'd love to become your first lady."

Chapter 23

"Small crowd tonight, huh?" Minta asked.

"Of all the things she could've said to me, this is what she chooses to say? Oh yes, tonight should be very interesting." Regina thought to herself.

Each event leading up to the family barbecue had been well attended, however, tonight's party was not.

If backyards reflect their owner's personalities, the Montgomery's backyard spoke well of them.

The few children that were there zipped in between the pool area where Regina and Minta stood, laughing and chasing one another.

"Be careful around the pool children." Mother Montgomery cautioned, taking notice of the mothers.

The decorative garden lanterns and blown glass glowed catching the sparks of the setting sun provided a warm glow.

The smells of grilled and smoked meats filled the evening air, question was, who was going to eat it?

Flashing a cold smile to show her insincerity, Regina replied, "Looks that way."

Stepping closer, Minta asked in an attempt towards reconciliation, "As usual, everything looks beautiful, is there anything I can do to help."

Straightening up the crisp table lines, Regina snapped back at Minta, "Nope, I think you've already done enough."

Regina continued to straighten things out despite realizing the crowd they'd planned for wasn't showing up. She also hurled mental insults towards Minta, "*Save your false humility for someone else because I'm not buying it. Had it not been for you, my party tonight wouldn't be ruined. My God, Scarlett and Carson aren't even here. People are now gossiping and talking about us and mostly everyone called and cancelled after what happened last night. And now you want to come and make nice and help?*" Regina thought.

Looking around searching for George, Minta saw him standing next to Bishop enjoying a glass of iced-tea and man to man conversation. She motioned to him to indicate things weren't going as well with Regina. Between Regina and Minta there was no steady stream of chatter and Minta was feeling the burn from the fallout from the night before.

George returned her motion with one to indicate to Minta to keep trying.

Responding internally to Regina's external emotions of displeasure, Minta took a deep breath, humbled herself and said, "Do you mind if we talk?"

Instead of facing Minta to respond, Regina turned her body at an angle and said slightly above a whisper, "I have nothing to say to you."

Still making observations, Mother Montgomery stood from her lounge chair when she heard Regina's sharp response.

"I've seen and heard enough, sit down you two." Mother Montgomery instructed.

Following Mother's orders, Minta and Regina sat down opposite one another.

Taking the lead, Mother Montgomery opened up with, "For years I've seen how a wedding, a funeral, and the birth of a baby can tear a family a part...if you let it. It seems like these kinds of events provides the most fertile breeding ground for conflicts but we're not going to give space to the enemy any more than what's already been done. Now, your children are about to be married and the two of you should be ashamed of yourselves as to how you've been carrying on. Y'all are better than this, you need to fix it."

Mother Montgomery scolded Regina and Minta as if they were two school aged girls who were sent to the principal's office.

She started out that way with them because she knew she would end building them up and loving them through their conflict.

Mother Montgomery schooled the two women with penetrating perception and wisdom directed exclusively for them. It was clear as to why she was the mother of the family.

"Marriage is a covenant or alliance between two families, the two of you are about to become a new family, let's get this thing figured out and start enjoying this happy time in all of our lives. The two of you are both powerful women of God so I don't need to tell you what the word says but I will. We should try to carefully preserve Christian love and peace with all brethren but in y'alls case, sisteren," Mother said chuckling, proud of her play on words. Turning serious again, she continued, "The coming of our Lord is near and if you know like I know you'll try to seek peace and do it without delay. It's time to stop all of this foolishness." Mother encouraged.

Cutting off Mother Montgomery as she spoke, Regina blared, "But what if I don't want to be a woman of God or a first lady right now? What if I want to be a mother who's angry, angry that this woman who doesn't think my son is good enough for her daughter, huh? I knew something was wrong with Minta the moment she got here. This woman had the nerve to come up in my house, in my church, in my family with some serious issues when I've been nothing but kind to her. She's only been concerned about herself and has not for once taken no one or nothing else into consideration."

Minta felt a dullness resting in her chest, she felt quite uncomfortable. The night air began to tease her skin after the sun had made its last appearance for the day, she was increasingly becoming uneasy. Regina's words stung but not as much as the mosquito that snacked on her for dinner.

"Ouch." Minta yelled and she swatted the mosquito from her arm.

Mother Montgomery raised up in her seat, "Well alright then, they always told me if you can't say amen then say ouch." Mother said snickering. "Looks like we might be getting somewhere here."

Regina sat with folded arms across her body, full of resentment, the pool candles she stared at seemed to calm her nerves somewhat. Given the fact she was the one who picked them out specifically for tonight's barbecue.

"Regina, God isn't going to mind that you have human emotions about things, what He is going to care about is how you choose to reconcile them. The bible says we are to confess our faults one to another and to pray for one another that you may be healed.[2]" Mother Montgomery rebuked. "So, who has something they'd like to confess?"

Minta's lips pressed together in a slight grimace, she still had the same feelings towards Carson but she'd begun to see and understand the full ramification of her disdain for him. Her feelings for him were hurting those she cared about instead of helping.

"Mother, I'd like to go first; I have something I'd like to say. First of all, I'd like to apologize for my behavior, Mother Montgomery, you're right, it wasn't Christ-like and I was wrong. I was in my feelings

---

[2] **James 5:16**: "Confess your faults one to another, and pray one for another, that ye may be healed. The effectual fervent prayer of a righteous man availeth much." **(KJV)**

about a lot of things and I let them get the best of me. I'm sorry and I ask you both for your forgiveness."

Mother Montgomery picked up Minta's hand to pat it in support of her admission. "Weddings are occasions for a time of great family rejoicing, what happened Minta to make you feel so upset to begin with? Why aren't you rejoicing dear, what's going on?" Mother Montgomery asked.

Looking at Regina and then Mother Montgomery before answering, Minta cleared her throat and said, "I'm sorry and I don't mean any harm but I just don't trust him."

While Regina was upset with the way Minta handled her frustrations and suspicions, truth be told, she didn't trust Carson either, so in some small way, she understood.

Both mothers wanted the best for their children, the problem was, their respective interpretations of what "best" meant.

Regina loosened up a bit and said, "Minta...mother to mother, I understand it may be hard to see your one and only daughter get married off and especially to someone who, as you've admitted, don't trust. This is the first time either one of us have had a child to get married so we've never had to navigate through something like this before. I'm sure when Scarlett left for college you may have cried but you knew she was transitioning but would always come back home. However, I'm sure her leaving home for marriage means something entirely different to you. But I want you to know, I love

Scarlett like my very own daughter, I love her, we all love her and even when you don't trust my son, you can trust me, we're going to take care of her. Carson may have his faults but Bishop and I are going to watch over them and help them along the way."

Minta slowly began to cry, Regina had addressed one of her core concerns and the acknowledgment opened a well of tears within her.

Regina and Minta talked out their issues and concerns and Mother Montgomery stood watch over them to assist in the reconciliation process.

Mother Montgomery stood to console Minta, rubbing her across the shoulders, Mother also grabbed Regina's hands and said, "See what happens when we talk things out and confess our hearts to one another? The other part of that scripture says we are to pray, the wedding is in two days so let's do that so the healing can begin."

Taking in a deep breath, with a bowed head, Mother Montgomery closed her eyes and began to pray, "Oh most precious and eternal Father, we ask You who loves mankind and is most merciful and compassionate, to have mercy upon us and our families. Father God, you established the family before the church and as such, we know that family matters to You. Lord, I pray for restoration and reconciliation; I pray for the restoration of Regina and Minta's relationship. Let them be the women and mothers you've called them to be in this season. Let them be an example of the word where it says we can love each other despite our differences. From the rising of the sun unto the going down of the same bless us with your unfailing love. Bind us together oh Lord with cords that cannot be broken, may we be led by those same cords towards kindness. Guide us with Your might, protect us with Your power, comfort us by Your spirit. Oh Lord, we call on You to be an ever-present help in our lives. And for all You're about to do my Lord, we give You the honor, glory, and praise. In Jesus' name we pray, Amen."

In unison, the trio all declared, "Amen."

With tears flowing from all three, Mother Montgomery pushed the envelope and her authority a step further, "Now, c'mon in and lets hug."

Without any hesitation, Regina and Minta both leaned in for the much-needed embrace.

"I'll try to do better if you will." Regina said to Minta with a weak smile.

Feeling compelled to humble herself, Minta said, apologizing, "So will I and Regina, I'm sorry."

Chapter 24

"I never would have imagined you were going to bring me here." Scarlett said laughing opening the door to Carson's car.

Running over to open Scarlett's door, Carson smiled and said, "Here, let me help you. Well this is the kind of stuff you can look forward to when we're married because I can be very unpredictable, I like being able to keep you guessing."

Reaching to retrieve Scarlett from the bucket seats of his car, Scarlett grinned as she watched the giant spinning Ferris wheel and the colorful looping roller coasters.

Listening to the roaring whirling of the rides and the squeals of people on them seemed to increase Scarlett's excitement for being in the electrifying atmosphere.

Locking arms with Scarlett, Carson leaned in, "Well, I figured since the Fall Carnival was only in town for a few more days, we should come and enjoy it before it leaves town. What do you think, did I choose well for our date night?"

Creepy clown laughter blared out from the static sounding speakers as Scarlett looked around smiling, "You've definitely chosen well tonight."

The traveling carnival was just what Scarlett needed, a break from all of the church sanctioned pre-wedding events.

Growing up, she always wanted tickets to the traveling fairs and carnivals but Minta didn't want their family to attend them because of her intense fear of clowns, she also felt like clowns were anti-Christian.

Every year the trucks would roll into town, Scarlett would get excited and hold out hope, thinking to herself, *"Maybe this year I'll get to go."*

If they were out at night and happened to ride by, Scarlett would ride in the backseat with her face smashed up against the window.

Feeling the papery ride tickets between her fingers took her back to those days, the feeling she felt opened her up to be thankful for the place in her life where she currently stood. Next to her fiancé' at the carnival. In that moment, something so simple meant the world to her.

"I'd like to think I've chosen well with you too sweetheart." Carson said smiling at Scarlett.

Trying to figure out which carnival food she'd try first, Scarlett was like a kid in a candy store, would she sample sweet and sticky candy apples, deep fried Oreos first, a funnel cake, elephant ears dusted with cinnamon and sugar, cotton candy, humongous turkey legs, or beer battered onion rings cooked in hot oil.

"Hmm, everything looks so delicious and I want to eat it all but I can't help but think about earlier years, my mother's words are ringing in my head, she always said, a minute on the lips, a lifetime on the hips and I have to fit in my wedding dress." Scarlett thought to herself.

Returning her attention back to Carson, "There's no need to think, I can assure you, you have chosen well Carson Montgomery." Scarlett confirmed, smiling from ear-to-ear.

Carson loved seeing the light shine from Scarlett's eyes as she took in all of the sights and sounds of the carnival.

With only two more nights left of the carnival funhouse, it was crowded with people trying to enjoy themselves before the fun left town again.

Being bumped from behind from someone in the crowd, the couple was face to face and seized the moment, they kissed under the flashing lightbulbs.

The moment they shared was sweet and endearing. As sweet as the traces of pink and blue cotton candy left on Scarlett's lips.

With Carson bringing Scarlett to the carnival, unbeknownst to him, he'd made a childhood dream come true. The feelings that caused her to initially fall for him were returning. Scarlett's thoughts of Gregory were slowly being pushed aside, where they belonged.

Without any one from the church surrounding them the couple had a chance to let their hair down and have some fun. They laughed, played games, enjoyed all types of artery clogging food but they loved every minute of it and in that moment, they were totally and completely in love with one another.

Chapter 25

"So, you look better this morning than you did yesterday morning. I'm guessing things are back to normal with you and Carson?" Sherry asked.

Nodding while speaking, Scarlett smiled and said, "Yes, things are back on track and back to normal."

"That must've been some date night last then huh?" Sherry joked.

"It was very nice, we talked, we laughed, we just hung out and it felt great. I think it was exactly what we needed to remind us of why we're here getting married this week." Scarlett said.

"Um, not just this week but you're getting married...tomorrow." Sherry reinforced.

Getting the giggles, Scarlett shrieked, "Yes, I know...the big day is...tomorrow."

Caught up in the joy and jubilation of her wedding day, Scarlett missed a call on her cell phone.

Seconds later, another call came through, along with a voice and text message.

"Girl, I think you may want to check your phone, it's going off like crazy over here." Sherry said.

Picking up the phone from the nightstand, Scarlett exclaimed, "Oh wow, Jennifer has called me like three times back to back. She sent me a text message too. Hmmm, let me see what she said."

Scarlett read Jennifer's message aloud to Sherry:

"This is some bull, you need to call me ASAP!"

"I wonder what that's about?" Sherry said.

Flipping through her phone, Scarlett scrolled to Jennifer's number and called her.

Jennifer Smith, Scarlett's old college roommate, they started out as roommates Freshman year and decided to stay together during their entire college career.

Jennifer along with Kelly Peters, a sorority sister of Scarlett's would serve as her bridesmaids.

A six-month pregnant Jennifer, highly upset when Scarlett returned her call, you could hear the frustration in her voice. "Girl, you better call your people and why didn't you answer me when I called you the first time?"

"Well hello to you too Jennifer. I saw your text, what's going on? Scarlett asked putting Jennifer on speaker phone.

Jennifer adjusted her phone to be able to yell in it, "So Kelly and I arrived at the airport and someone from the church picked us up and brought us to the bridal salon for our final fitting, right?"

"Right." Scarlett replied.

"Well, this woman from the church is now saying I'm not allowed to participate in the wedding because I've gone against the bridesmaid's contract." Jennifer shouted.

"Bridesmaids contract?" Both Scarlett and Sherry exclaimed.

"Yes, this woman, I think her name is Sylvia or something said, the contract specifically states bridesmaids cannot drastically change their look before the wedding." Jennifer shouted.

"Why am I just now hearing about this? Did you sign a contract Jennifer? Scarlett asked.

"I guess I did but I didn't know that's what it was. I hate to admit it but I didn't read the darn thing. I saw it in my email, just figured it was related to regular bridal party duties and I signed it." Jennifer replied.

"I did too Scarlett, I did the same thing." Kelly chimed in.

Tilting her head to the side and pursing her lips, Sherry revealed, "I didn't receive a contract, I don't know anything about this."

"This Sylvia woman said since you were family, they didn't send you one, only me and Kelly got it and then we didn't even read the thing." Jennifer admitted.

"So, I guess now, what's the problem? Why is she saying you can't be in the wedding?" Scarlett asked.

"Girl, you know I've been waiting and waiting and all of a sudden my baby bump just popped out. The way things were looking, I didn't think it would show up right before your wedding. Now my dress doesn't fit, it's too tight...I'm sorry Scarlett. She said that the weddings at their church follow a set of procedures and set processes and that everything has to be in a certain way, with a certain look." Jennifer explained.

Scarlett squealed, "You have a baby bump, you've started showing? Ahh, I can't wait to see you and listen, you have nothing to be sorry for."

Speaking over Jennifer, Kelly said, "My dress fits perfectly Scarlett so I'm good. I think I may need to read back over that contract though.

"Scarlett, focus...there's a serious issue here. If what Jennifer and Kelly are saying is true, you need to do something because this church looks like they don't play." Directing her conversation towards Scarlett's phone, Sherry asked, "Can either one of you email me a copy of that contract so I can take a look at it?"

"I'm pulling it up now Sherry, I'll send it to you in just a second." Kelly offered.

Tapping her fingers against her lips, Scarlett suggested, "Hey, why don't guys leave there. Have who ever took you there bring you here and I'll see about getting this all worked out."

Ending the call, Scarlett screamed, "Just when I was getting back excited about getting married, this mess pops up, who makes bridesmaids sign a contract, who does that? This is utterly ridiculous."

"What's ridiculous is the stuff in this agreement. No major hair changes, no wigs, I will not out do the bride in anyway, I will not knowingly or unknowingly get pregnant more than three months prior to the wedding, no advances towards any male guests attending, I mean this list goes on and on. I can see why they didn't read it, I'm sure they thought this was a joke, a prank from you and your silly self." Sherry said.

Leaning up against the wall, Scarlett's shoulders drooped, "This is insane, what should I do Sherry?"

Sherry opened her mouth to speak and then closed it, scratching her cheek, she tried again, "Maybe this would be a good time to call your mom. She knows more about these church people and their protocols than I do."

Theatrical groaning emerged from Scarlett, "I was hoping you'd have something more than that. I'm not calling her, what else you got?" Scarlett said.

"If you don't want to call your mom for advice, listen up, try and see if you can talk to whoever is in charge and created this monster of a contract. Hopefully, it's possible to come to a peaceable resolve. If not, I'll take a closer look at it and see if I can speak with the church's counsel to see if we can work something out." Sherry said shaking her head. "I've never seen anything like this in my life, let me know what you decide to do because my honey will be here soon and I'm ready to see him too."

"Okay, I'll probably go see who I can talk to before Jennifer and Kelly get here. Well, with Glenn arriving today, I guess I won't see you until later at the rehearsal, huh?" Scarlett asked.

"Yeah, you're probably right because I need to tie up a few loose ends for later, boy, do I have a surprise for you." Sherry said.

Chapter 26

"Man, that shot was ugly." Carson said to himself.

Taking inventory of the remaining balls on the exquisite oak pool table, Carson realized his focus was off. Balancing himself on a bar stool, Carson took aim at another ball, stopping briefly, he cued up his stick and said, "C'mon, bank shot baby."

Carson's ball stopped shy of the corner pocket, he was about to get upset with himself until he heard, "Hey, there you are. I've been calling you man, why aren't you answering me?" Kevin asked.

"What do you want Kevin?" Carson asked.

"Uh, hello Kevin, how are you? I'm fine, thanks for asking." Kevin mocked.

Chalking his pool cue again, Carson scanned the table and said, "What's up with you man, I'm trying to focus on my game man."

"That's what I'm here to talk to you about, your game...the bachelor party tonight is going to be crazy ignorant, everything is all set." Kevin said bouncing from one foot to the next.

Glancing at the flat screen attached to the wall, taking in the latest sports news, Carson casually said, "I'm sorry but I'm not going."

Kevin's bouncing came to a complete halt.

"What do you mean you aren't going, you know I've been planning this for weeks now." Kevin declared.

"Yeah, I know and I'm sorry...well, I'm sorry but I'm not really." Carson replied.

"Sorry ain't going to cut it man, what gives? Where's all this coming from?" Kevin asked.

Putting down the pool stick, Carson walked around to the minibar and grabbed a bottle of water. "What gives is that I'm getting married tomorrow and it's time for me to start acting like it. It's about time I put my grown man on. Little boys seek side chicks and play games but real men seek wives and I've found mine." Carson explained.

Kevin's head flinched back slightly, "What?" Kevin asked in a state of befuddlement.

"You heard me, I didn't stutter. After the rehearsal and the dinner, I'm going to relax and get myself ready to marry my lady tomorrow. I'll probably consecrate myself too."

Walking towards the door, Kevin said, "I think I need to walk out and come back in again, maybe, things will be different when I come back. I feel like I'm in the Twilight Zone, especially with Carson talking about consecration. What am I going to tell the boys, they were looking forward to this?"

"When you come back, things will be the same and I don't care what you tell the guys, my mind is made up." Carson declared.

With his back to the door, Carson didn't realize that things were actually different as he walked back in. He wasn't alone.

"So, what am I supposed to tell all of the guys expecting a night on the town tonight?" Kevin asked.

Mildly irritated, Carson turned to yell at Kevin but in return, the words fell out of his mouth and it dropped to the floor in surprise.

Carson's brothers, Cayden-James and Christian stood together smiling at their big brother's surprised face.

Carson's eyes widened as he looked at his brothers standing in front of him, "What, wait, how did you guys get here; I thought with the mission trip and all, you weren't going to be able to make it." Carson said.

The youngest Montgomery son stepped to the oldest son and said, "There was no way in the world we'd miss your big day. We flew all night but we're here, congratulations man, tomorrow's the big day huh?"

Pulling his two brothers in for a hug, Carson was at a loss for words. He'd made peace with the fact their mission trip would cause them to miss the wedding.

"So, you ready for tomorrow big bro? How's wedding week been for you, has it been crazy?" Christian asked.

"Dude, wedding week has been crazy, before I go into all of that, I want to know about the mission trip." Carson said.

Jumping in to the brotherly conversation, Kevin shouted, "Man, y'all can catch up later. I'm still trying to figure out what to do about this bachelor party?"

"What about it?" Christian inquired.

"Carson's not going." Kevin replied.

Cayden-James and Christian looked at Carson and erupted in laughter, "What do you mean this guy here's not going to his own bachelor party? That is hilarious." Cayden-James said.

"Hey listen, you guys can laugh all you want but I've done enough partying to last me a lifetime. I'm hanging up my player card, no more games. I've had enough time living the single life, I'm trying to make a change and do better. I need to do better for myself and definitely do better by my future wife. Going out tonight will only complicate things for me so I'm going to stay in." Carson acknowledged.

"Sounds like Carson's ready to leave, cleave and weave around here." Christian said jokingly.

Leaning in closer to Carson, Cayden-James placed his hand on Carson's shoulders and said, 'I'm proud of you man, that's awesome if you really mean what you just said."

Being the baby of the family, throughout Cayden-James' life, no matter what Carson did, he only saw him as his big brother and he adored him. Unlike Christian, Cayden-James held an ability to look past Carson's mistakes and still yet look up to him.

"I meant every word; I'm a changed man guys." Carson said.

Collapsing onto the cushy, leathered couch, Kevin offered, "Well, I'm glad you've made peace and changed and all but I think I've decided, who cares if you aren't going, anyone who wants to roll with me tonight, can. I'm not cancelling the party, we're still going to have a good time, with or without you Carson."

Having faith in his own ability and decision, Carson replied, "Do your thing man, have fun, and be safe out there. I need you guys to be on point tomorrow."

Looking around to see where the old Carson was, Kevin replied pointing towards Carson, "Man, who is this guy?"

Cayden-James and Christian laughed as Carson approached Kevin with ease, "Don't ever question who I am or anything else about me, I'm Carson Eugene Montgomery IV and don't you ever forget it."

Chapter 27

"I hope everyone's on time for this wedding rehearsal." Regina said checking the time.

"Oh sweetheart, you need to stop worrying so much. Everything is going to work out how it's supposed to." Bishop said.

Fingering her pearl necklace, "With everything that's been going on, I just feel like now, with each passing day and every event we have, it feels like the hammer is about to fall on us. Lord knows I keep praying asking Him to help us just get to tomorrow, Jesus."

"Regina."

"Eugene, you didn't hear the way Scarlett called me today upset about her bridesmaids...did you know they were asked to sign a bridesmaid's contract?" Regina asked.

Laughing heartily, Bishop replied, "No, I didn't know that but I guess the staff felt like one was needed. I don't busy myself with details like that."

Seated on the edge of her husband's desk, Regina leaned in and said, "Have you busied yourself with speaking with your son?"

Bishop's laughter was quieted with Regina's question, "Honey, I have not but I will. I haven't spoken to him but Mother told me she has and he's good."

"The wedding's tomorrow Eugene, when do you plan to speak with him?" Regina inquired.

Taking Regina by the hand, Bishop Montgomery lifted her up and hugged her, "You need to learn how to let things happen, you're not going to be able to control everything Regina. All this here is wedding stuff, what I want to make sure is that they understand after the wedding, there's a marriage. I'll speak with him Regina but listen, no matter what happens, good or bad, I'm going to be here with you. This is a happy time for our family. Let's act like there's a reason to celebrate, our son's getting married." Bishop cheered.

Inside the sanctuary, the event planning staff was busy, moving around like tiny worker bees accepting deliveries and setting the stage for one of the biggest weddings to hit Vino, California.

The wood polished pews were receiving an extra coat of shine as the staffers attached pew decorations.

There were staffers on each aisle that separated the pews into sections.

The communion table was being prepped as well as the sound systems and instruments were being tuned up.

A full-on transformation was taking place right before Regina's eyes as she peered through the window of her husband's office that led into the sanctuary.

A mixture of emotions engulfed her, she was happy and excited but worried and nervous at the same time.

Opening the door to Bishop's office, Cayden-James and Christian walked in.

"Hey, hey, hey...we're back." Christian said smiling.

"Did you miss us?" Cayden-James asked.

Seeing her other two sons who'd made it home safely was a relief, calling out as a release of her inner struggles, she yelled, "Praise the Lord, my boys are home. Thank you, Jesus." Reaching in to hug them, Regina touched them both with shaky hands, "Let me look at you two. I want to make sure this is real, I'm so glad to have you both back home."

Boasting a satisfied smile, Bishop Montgomery stood up, he stood tall and said, "Welcome home boys, it's good to have you back. From everything I've heard, the mission trip was a success and I'm proud of the work you guys did over there."

"Yeah Bishop, it was an awesome time and we're glad to be home and especially glad to be here in time for Carson's wedding." Cayden-James expressed.

Breaking her embrace, Regina walked back over to the glass window looking inside the sanctuary and said, "Yes, the wedding."

"Are you okay mother?" Christian asked.

With her eyes fixated on the work being done, Regina answered, "I'm fine son, there's just a lot going on."

Checking himself out in the mirror in his father's office, Christian ran his fingers through his hair and said, "So we've heard."

"From who? Who told you what's happened?" Regina inquired.

"Oh, we went by to see grandma before we came here and she told us." Cayden-James answered.

"And so what do you guys think?" Regina asked.

"I'm not surprised by what I heard." Christian said.

"I heard what she said but I also heard what Carson said and I think he's through with all of that stuff. I think he's ready to settle down." Cayden-James believed.

Chapter 28

"Are you going to be alright mom? I mean you still haven't spoken to Scarlett?" Cole asked.

"No, I haven't spoken to her and yes, I'll be fine. If she's open to it, I plan to talk to her and apologize, I'm going to apologize to Carson as well." Minta said.

"Oh wow, now there's a switch." Cole replied.

Strolling into the sanctuary with her bridal party in tow along with their respective significant others, Scarlett was radiant. The wedding rehearsal dress she'd chosen to wear was a perfect fit for her. Fashioned in lace, mesh, and beads, the dress possessed an illusion yoke of a neckline that all together offered a polished look that wore well over Scarlett's petite frame.

Standing at the door waiting, George took a gasp as he saw Scarlett enter, "Breathtaking, you look beautiful honey."

Greeting her father, Scarlett smiled and said, "Thank you daddy."

Taking inventory of Scarlett's clique, George smiled and said, "Oh hi ladies, Jennifer and Kelly, hi guys, glad to see you all made it in. It's so nice to see you again." Taking a step back, George held out his hand, "Glenn, my man. Nice to see you son."

Being the father figure in Sherry's life, George was the one who'd grill all of the Sherry's boyfriends, the serious ones at least. She wasn't allowed to go past three dates without first having George meet them.

Not only did he like Glenn but he honored him by granting him his blessing when he came and asked for Sherry's hand in marriage.

Having her friends and family with her Scarlett was ready to rehearse, things were starting to click again. She was able to get the dress situation worked out. The seamstress at the bridal salon was able to work her magic and Jennifer was able to wear her dress without any issues.

She and Carson had gone out on an ice cream date, they were back in a good place and Gregory had stopped calling and texting.

Things were great.

Well, not quite.

She still hadn't spoken to her mother.

The Montgomery family walked into the sanctuary to greet all who had arrived.

Introductions were made, hugs and kisses were exchanged, and smiles were shared. Scarlett and Carson were thrilled to be surrounded by family and friends that believed in their love and wanted to be there to support them. They were ready to celebrate with people they both loved and cared for.

Minta sat and watched everyone from the front where she was seated.

Feeling a tapping on her shoulder, Minta turned to hear Mother Montgomery whispering in her ear, "Ain't no need in you sitting back and watching from the sidelines. Get in the game, Mother of the Bride."

"Places everyone. We need to do a full run through the entire ceremony." The head wedding planner said.

"The entire ceremony." Everyone seemed to ask all together.

"Maybe we can just go over the real important parts." Regina suggested.

Most often, Regina's suggestions were thinly veiled decrees and everyone knew it.

Standing on the stage with her tablet in hand and wireless mic attached to her, the wedding planner said, "That's fine, whatever you want First Lady. I still need for everyone to line up so we can get started."

Everyone was in place and the wedding rehearsal was in full swing.

If the rehearsal was any indication to how the main event was to play out, Carson and Scarlett were in trouble.

Any and everything that could go wrong...did. The unity candles wouldn't light, the flower girls and ring bearers refused to walk down the aisle and participate. The van from the florist delivering the flowers was struck by another car and the driver was rushed to the hospital by way of ambulance. People who had absolutely nothing to do with the wedding or the planning now all of sudden had opinions and ideas.

With each interruption, the wind in Scarlett's sail got weaker and weaker.

Touching her temple, Scarlett let her eyes close so the tears that were gathering wouldn't fall.

"Is this a sign? Are ALL of these things happening signs? Lord, are you trying to tell me this is a mistake?" Scarlett thought.

Noticing, Mother Montgomery said from her seat, "It's okay baby, sometimes the bad moments make the best memories."

Despite the rounds and rounds of missteps and mishaps going on with the rehearsal, Carson was snapping pictures and presenting a much different story on social media, giving his followers a behind the scenes look at his wedding rehearsal.

He was enjoying himself and the social support he was receiving with each post.

Unfortunately, there was one follower who didn't share in the joy.

With each post, Michelle fumed.

Her battle plan at the comedy show didn't work out how she planned but tonight, unwilling to consider the consequences, she prepared for war.

Given all of the issues surrounding the wedding, the rehearsal seemed to drag on.

The bridal party started to get anxious and everyone's mind shifted to eating at the rehearsal dinner.

At the close of the rehearsal, everyone there with a cellphone and connected to Carson received an email.

One by one, they checked their phones.

The subject line read: **I'm Getting Married.**

Christian, one of the first to check his phone said, "Hey man, why are you emailing us, everyone knows you're getting married."

"What are you talking about Christian, I've been here rehearsing with everyone here, how could I have sent an email?" Carson asked.

"I don't know, maybe you scheduled to send one out, who knows, it came from your email address." Christian confirmed.

A sinking feeling washed over Regina, rushing to check her phone on the pew in front of her, she saw the email Christian was referring to. Her trembling hands clicked the email to read its contents.

"On this Saturday, October 19th, I'm getting married but before I do I need to let you all know that I'm a slime dog, whore-heifer from hell. I'm a liar and the truth does not agree with me. I love to make women love me and then leave them high and dry. So, before I take on a wife tomorrow, I wanted you all to know the truth about me."

Attached to the email were inappropriate pictures of Carson.

Michelle's first casualty of war was Regina, mortified by the contents of the email, her phone fell to the ground and cracked.

"Wait, what does the email say?" Scarlett asked looking at Carson.

Before Carson could answer, the wedding planner ran up to the stage and cautioned Bishop Montgomery. She pulled him aside and showed him her tablet.

"Sir, this thing is getting worse and worse by the minute. The church has alerts set up on each of you so when someone posts something online using your names, the church gets notified. I was just informed by the church to check out what's happening under Carson's name and it's not good." The wedding planner shared.

The one-time Carson had gone to Michelle's house, he'd left some clothes behind. In addition, he asked her to send out an email for him from her computer while he charged his phone. While looking at his social media posts at the wedding rehearsal, she remembered the clothes and his login credentials and went to work.

"Here's an EBay auction entitled, Carson Montgomery's Dirty Laundry, someone has created a profile on here and is supposedly selling Carson's clothes. The ad says, here's your chance to air Carson Montgomery's dirty laundry or shall I say, here's your chance to wear his dirty laundry. As you can see here, someone has created a website, *"Preacher's Kids Gone Wild,"* it's not the best showing of Carson either sir. There are all kinds of things popping up in forums and all over the Internet about Carson sir." The wedding planner added.

Bishop felt a pain in the back of his mouth, he felt it was resulting from the words he hadn't yet spoken to Carson.

Bishop Montgomery's eyes squinted as he watched the events of Carson's bad judgement unfold right in the middle of the church he was soon to turn over to him.

Leaning over to the wedding planner, Bishop gave sharp instructions, "Get our tech team on this and shut it down now. Plus, make sure our security team has more bodies in place tomorrow for the wedding."

Crushed by the contents in her phone, Scarlett looked at Carson and said, "I'm done."

Walking away Carson ran behind her, "Scarlett wait, baby, I didn't do this. I know you're upset but let's take some time and work this out. Can't you tell someone is trying to bring me down?"

Snatching her arm from Carson's grip, Scarlett yelled, "Get your hands off of me Carson."

Sherry, Jennifer, and Kelly quickly gathered their things and hurried out behind Scarlett.

"Hey wait up." Sherry called behind Scarlett.

Stopping for the ladies to catch up, Scarlett looked at Sherry and said, "Wherever and whatever you were planning to do for me tonight, take me there now, I need a drink."

Chapter 29

"Scarlett?" Kelly said. "Scarlett, did you hear what I said?"

Slamming down another shot, Scarlett motioned and yelled, "I said I don't want to talk about it."

The neon and strobe lights bounced around the club, inside the V.I.P. area of the multi-level nightclub, Scarlett reached for another lime wedge off of the glowing tray of drinks, as she sat in the middle of her bachelorette party.

"Shout outs to Scarlett celebrating her last night as a free woman." The DJ announced over the loud speaker.

"So this is what you've been planning all week?" Scarlett asked with slurred speech. "You thought I'd like coming to and spend my last night as a free woman at a club? Well...you're right." Scarlett yelled throwing her hands up in the air.

Dancing with strangers sharing the same V.I.P. section, Scarlett pushed her hair to the side to hear the guy she was dancing with say, "Hey, let's take a picture together."

"Sure, let's do it." Scarlett replied.

Jennifer, in her ever-pregnant state, realized banging loud music and large crowds was no longer a picture of fun for her. Her baby was overreacting to the music, leaning over to Kelly, she said, "I think I'm getting ready to go, it's been a long day and I need to get some rest and who knows how tomorrow is going to turn out."

"I hear you on that Jennifer, I'm ready to go too but I'm worried about Scarlett. Clubs, partying like this, drinking, cursing...when did she start that? This isn't her at all, none of this is and she won't talk about what happened back at the church." Kelly said.

"I don't know and I'm too sleepy to try and figure it out, I guess when she's ready to talk to us, she will. Let's tell Sherry we're leaving." Jennifer explained.

Walking towards Sherry, Jennifer and Kelly said, "Hey, I think we're going to head out, we're ready to get to our hotel, we'll call a cab or something but we're just so tired, we'll see you in the morning."

"Are we getting ready at the Montgomery's house or at the church and what time should we be there?" Kelly asked.

"Did you guys forget about the bridal breakfast? Be at the Montgomery house at 7:30, bright and early." Sherry said discussing the details of the next day.

"Okay Sherry, we'll be there." Jennifer answered. "I'm just tired, we'll see you tomorrow."

Hugging Scarlett's friends, Sherry said, "Okay, that's fine, have a good night and I'll see you tomorrow morning."

Distracted by dancing and taking selfies with strangers, Scarlett didn't see members of her bridal party disappear in the dim light of the club.

Checking for a signal on her phone, Sherry smiled when she saw what she was looking for.

Scarlett's surprise had arrived.

"May I cut in this dance please?" Sherry asked placing herself between Scarlett and her dancing buddy.

"It's time to go, time to move on to the next thing." Sherry instructed.

Checking their table, Scarlett asked, "Where did Jennifer and Kelly go?"

"They left already and it's time for us to go to. C'mon."

A line of people snaked the building outside of the establishment still waiting to be let in.

Stepping outside into the night air cleared Scarlett's head up somewhat.

However, it wasn't until she saw Gregory step in from out of the shadows that she quickly sobered up.

Approaching Scarlett and Sherry, Scarlett grabbed Sherry's arm, "What is he doing here? Did you know about this?"

"Surprise." Sherry said smiling.

"Surprise my behind. Sherry, what were you thinking, this is not a good idea...at all." Scarlett shrieked.

Before Gregory made his way to them, Sherry looked at Scarlett, "It's obvious to me you have some unfinished business here, I told you to handle it, and now you have a chance to." Sherry declared.

"Hello ladies." Gregory said approaching.

"Am I still drunk or is he is incredibly overly handsome right now?" Scarlett screamed to herself.

Reaching in for a hug, Gregory looked at Scarlett and said, "I hear congratulations are in order beautiful. Congratulations."

Gregory was wearing the same cologne she met him in, his smelled tickled her nose. The heat from his clothed body next to hers made her shiver.

"This isn't happening to me right now." Scarlett screamed again to herself.

"Thanks for calling me Sherry. If only for a night, I'm glad I get to see my sweet Scarlett for one last time before she gets married." Gregory said.

Dialing in a request for a ride share on her phone, "No problem Gregory, I'm glad you could make it. I'm about to get out of here. Now don't you two do anything I wouldn't do, oh who am I kidding, do what you feel you need to." Sherry said giggling.

Even in the night winds, Scarlett was visibly sweating, "You're leaving?" Scarlett exclaimed.

Sherry's ride pulled up and she waved good-bye getting into the car, "Yes, I am. Have a wonderful night."

Scarlett's muscles jumped under her skin.

"Sooo, now what?" Gregory asked.

Chapter 30

"Minta, why are you up so early, where are you going?" George asked half-asleep.

Gliding her feet into a pair of slippers, Minta whispered, "Go back to sleep George; I'll be back."

Grabbing her bible, Minta made her way out of the door.

Directly to the right of the guest house was the Montgomery's garden, it was more like an edible forest. The precious space on the property was aptly called, The Garden of Eden. It was one of Bishop's pet projects. He started it with one idea to illustrate that whatever you sow, it must grow and that whatever you plant, it will produce. However, in planting one thing, he developed green thumbs and continued to plant. Now, the majority of the fruit, herbs, and veggies were now supplied from Bishop's garden.

Following the stepping stones peeking up through the grass, Minta used the flashlight on her phone to lead her to a place to sit. Snipping off a piece of mint, Minta realized within a few more footsteps, she'd found a park bench.

Having a desire to pray and connect, Minta felt she needed to become one with nature as she went before the Lord.

"Father God, I offer you thanksgiving on this morning for the beauty and magnificence of the earth you've created. I thank you God for the trees and the flowers and the songs sung by the birds, I thank you for the morning dew that rests on the ground and in my heart. I thank you oh Lord. Now Father God, You've said in your word that I can come boldly before the throne of grace, where I will receive mercy and find grace to help me in my time of need and Lord, I'm in need. Your word says, you sympathize with my weaknesses and Lord I'm weak.[3]"

Opening her bible and her heart, Minta raised her hands and continued to cry out before the Lord, "I'm here to cry aloud and spare not, I'm calling out my own sin and transgressions God. I don't want to get so close to heaven and then miss it. Help me Lord. I've risen early, before the sun, crying out for help and I'm putting my hope in Your words. I don't want to be right about Carson but Lord help me to love him in spite of. Help me to be the believer you've called me to be, to cover him, to encourage him, and to build him up. I don't want to be this bitter old mother-in-law. Lord I need for You to make a way for me, create a way for me to be able to apologize to not only my daughter but to Carson as well. I'm calling on you Father, I'm making my requests made known to You through prayer and supplication with thanksgiving. I need you Lord, now like I've never needed you before. In Jesus' name I pray. Amen."

---

[3] **Hebrews 4:15-16**: "For we do not have a high priest who is unable to sympathize with our weaknesses, but we have one who was tempted in every way that we are, yet was without sin. Let us then approach the throne of grace with confidence, so that we may receive mercy and find grace to help us in our time of need." (**KJV**)

Before The Sun

The sun's rays started to prick the sky.

Minta's face glistened with tears.

Closing her bible, she wiped her face, closed her bible and dug her feet deep into soil beneath her. She sat motionless listening to the songs and chirping of the birds.

Chapter 31

"Did we have to get up at the butt-crack of dawn, sweetie?" Glenn asked with a slight hint of protest.

Sherry, the early riser, the morning person of the two smiled and said, "Yes, honey; I wanted us to talk and hang out a little before all of the festivities started...if they start." Sherry said, whispering that last part under her breath.

"How'd it go last night? That was crazy what happened at the church huh?" Glenn asked pouring a cup of coffee.

The gurgle of the hot tub roared as Sherry and Glenn sat on the edge with their feet submerged.

Glenn wasn't in on Sherry's plan to reconnect Gregory and Scarlett, for had he known, he would have never agreed.

"Last night was fun, the other two bridesmaids left a little early though. They all should be getting here soon for the breakfast." Sherry said.

"So what do you want to talk to me about?" Glenn asked.

Taking a sip of coffee, Sherry circled her feet in the hot tub, "Well, I wanted to see what you thought about something. After being here all week with these "church folk," I'm starting to question a few things." Sherry admitted.

"Hey listen, just because you put the church in front of their name means nothing, church folks are still plain 'ole folk. People in the church are subjected to the same desires and flaws as others." Glenn cautioned.

Having grown up in the church, Glenn carried a different perspective than Sherry who unlike Glenn did not grow up around ministry.

"I just feel like I've seen more drama with these people than I ever would have imagined. Not to mention, I think they probably missed an opportunity to win me over to their side. I mean I didn't grow up around it and I don't feel like I need to have church in my life now if it's going to be like this." Sherry confessed.

"Well sweetheart, that's where you are wrong. The problem is, you're looking at people and not Christ. As my mother used to always say, people are fickle but God is faithful. Given the chance, man will fail you but God never will. You need to take your eyes off of the faults of people and look to the redemptive power of Christ." Glenn admonished. "Church folk, as you call them have issues just like everyone else, they just choose to put their trust and faith in a Savior with hopes of doing better and being better people as a result of that commitment."

"Hmm, I guess I never really thought of it in that way." Sherry said nodding.

Kissing Sherry on the cheek, "I know, that's why you have me." Glenn said jokingly. "You said you were questioning things, what else is on your mind babe?"

Feeling unsure as to how Glenn would respond, Sherry cleared her throat, rubbing her forearms, "Well, the other thing that's been on my mind is that, seeing all of this going on this past week, I don't think I want to go through all of the trouble of a big wedding. What do you think about eloping?" Sherry asked. The real question she wanted to ask, she threw out quickly, "Or we could get married today?"

Glenn quickly glanced at Sherry, then turned his attention away and turned it towards the hot tub. "You want to elope, you want to get married today? But what about all of the planning you've already done for our wedding that's next month Sherry?"

"I don't care about any of that stuff, I'll call and cancel what I can get cancelled and what I can't, well, it is what it is but at least I'll have my peace of mind, instead of going crazy. I mean, we already have the marriage license, a wedding is happening today, we can just walk up right behind them. My aunt can marry us or I can even ask Bishop Montgomery to do it. I really don't care, all I know is, you're the most important person to me and I'm ready to make us official." Sherry explained.

Grabbing Sherry's hand, Glenn said, "I would have married you months ago but you wanted to have this fantastic wedding. I'm not sure how I feel about getting married today or eloping only for the simple fact that my parents won't be here. However, what you should know Sherry is that I love you and I will marry you any day, anytime, anywhere you want to." Glenn declared.

Chapter 32

"Today is supposed to be my wedding day and I can't even get my bride to talk to me." Carson gushed.

Pounding his fists onto his table, he checked his phone once again.

Nothing.

Well at least there was nothing from Scarlett.

His voicemail was full but he didn't care.

There were unanswered text messages but he didn't care about those either.

Doing what he knew to do, Carson, fell to his knees and began to petition the Lord. "Heavenly Father, who is almighty in power, love and strength, here am I at your feet, guilty as charged. Lord, my understanding is darkened and my sense of right and wrong are corrupted. Father God, please, open the eyes of my understanding and purify my heart and mind. I want to be the man You've called me to be; I want to be the husband Scarlett deserves and that my parents expect. Forgive me Father for I have sinned, wash me and cleanse me to where sin will leave no stain."

Traces of the sun began to flicker across the horizon, hinting towards its pending arrival, Carson, stowed away in his secret apartment in town, laid himself prostrate on the vintage, lightly-toned area rug. He buried his tear-stained face onto the floor.

"I'm a wretch undone seeking your redemption and I pray You don't withhold it from me. I need You to be for me what I can't be to myself. I've fallen short of Your glory; will you restore me oh Lord? I love Scarlett, I need her and I pray she'll find it in her heart to forgive me. Lord, if you do this for me; I'll be better, I promise to do better. To the only wise God, our Savior, be glory and majesty, forever and ever. Amen."

All over the Montgomery estate and abroad voice prints made towards heaven were being made regarding Carson, Scarlett, and their wedding.

Even where she was, Scarlett said a little prayer too.

Chapter 33

"Good morning, did you ladies get some rest last night?" Sherry asked.

"Yes, thank goodness. I feel much better this morning." Jennifer said nibbling on a muffin.

"I do too." Kelly replied. "Has anyone heard from Scarlett, shouldn't she be down here now?"

Now that Glenn was in town, Sherry had gone to his room instead of the one she'd been sharing with Scarlett so she was unaware Scarlett had not returned from the night before.

"Let me see if I can reach her." Sherry replied.

"Where are you and why aren't you here? You're late to your own bridal breakfast, your mom and mother-in-law are on their way, what are you doing?" Sherry asked.

Yawning, Scarlett replied, "I'm on my way."

"On your way from where, what've you been doing?" Sherry desired to know.

"Take me off of the witness stand Sherry, you reminded me I had unfinished business, you told me to handle said unfinished business and I did." Scarlett replied.

"And what does that mean?" Sherry said probing.

Before Scarlett could answer, someone assisting with the bridal breakfast called out, "Where's Scarlett, we need Scarlett."

"Um, well you need to hurry up and get here and handle some stuff because someone is asking for you. Hold on, let me see what's going on?" Sherry said.

Placing Scarlett on hold, Sherry turned with a smile and asked, "Uh, who's asking for Scarlett, where's she needed?"

"Bishop Montgomery is asking to see Scarlett." The assistant replied.

Turning her attention back to Scarlett, Sherry said, "Girl, your father-in-law is asking for you, how far out are you?

Scarlett felt a prickling of her scalp, time seemed to slow down as she tried to measure how far away she was from the Montgomery estate.

"Sherry, you need to stall for me. I'm only like two or three minutes away but I need to change my clothes, I don't need them to see me in the same ones I had on last night." Scarlett stated.

"Okay, I got you...the same clothes you had on from last night. Ooo, this is so scandalous. I can't wait to hear about what happened last night but for right now, hurry up and get here quickly. Especially before your mother comes for the breakfast and sees that you're not here. They're saying, Bishop Montgomery wants to see you in his office here at the house. Hurry up Scarlett." Sherry confirmed.

"I'm trying Sherry and you need to find me a way to get inside the house without anyone seeing me." Scarlett demanded.

"Can I feed you, burp you, and change your diaper, your highness?" Sherry asked sarcastically.

In a heightened and rushed tone, Scarlett replied, "I'm almost there just do what I asked, come help me out. Bye."

Ending her call with Scarlett, Sherry walked back over to the table with the rest of the bridal party and sat back down with all eyes on her from those waiting for answers.

Mustering up a hearty laugh, Sherry explained choosing her words carefully, "Scarlett will be down in a moment, silly thing, she appears to have overslept and is now trying to get herself together." Looking at the woman asking for Scarlett's behalf, Sherry smiled to her and said, "She knows Bishop is asking for her, she'll head to his office shortly."

Leaning in, Jennifer whispered to Sherry, "So what's really going on, you were on the phone with her way to long for her to have overslept. Is there even going to be a wedding today Sherry?"

"Shh, let's not talk about this here. Who knows what's about to happen but our job whether there will be one or not is to be here for her." Sherry instructed. "If she has to now go to Bishop Montgomery, given that, I actually think we should finish this breakfast early. More than anything, I don't want her mom and his mom to come down and see that she's not here. You ladies are welcomed to stay here or hang out somewhere until it's time for us to get ready. I'm going to excuse myself for a bit."

Chapter 34

"I've been up all night. Would you happen to know why?" Bishop Montgomery asked.

Lowering his head, Carson offered sighing, "Probably trying to fix this mess I'm in."

Bishop's pained expression added to the sleep lines or lack thereof, in his face.

"I'm trying to wait before Scarlett gets here but before she does I need to know; do you have any idea as to the amount of damage you've caused?" Bishop asked.

Biting at his lip, Carson simply held his head down and said, "I'm sorry Bishop, it was never my intention to cause so much trouble."

Bishop, not one to ever exhibit bouts of anger or fits of rage but today, he was different. The situation with Carson had caused a streak of righteous indignation to rise up within him. The kind like Jesus had when he drove out the money lenders from the temple.

"You're sorry? That's all you have to say is that you're sorry? Let me ask you something Carson, did it ever occur to you how much of an impact this would have on your mother, Scarlett, the Watsons, huh? Did it ever occur to you how this would bring such grave reproach on the church, myself, and not to mention, you?" Bishop proposed.

In an attempt to try and explain, Carson opened his mouth but his father still had words that needed to come from his.

"Carson, your mother and I had plans to start transitioning you into the Senior pastor role next year but given what has happened with you in this latest stunt, there is no way that is going to happen." Bishop Montgomery scolded.

A knock at the door interrupted his closed-door rebuke.

"Come in, it's open." Bishop proclaimed.

Looking somewhat refreshed, Scarlett entered.

Unsure as to what she was about to walk into, Scarlett's eyes narrowed, as if in confusion upon seeing Carson in front of his father.

Standing to greet Scarlett, Bishop Montgomery reached in for a hug and said, "Good morning sweetheart, thank you for coming to my office this morning."

Carson also stood.

Scarlett circled him in a round-about fashion, with a weak smile and sat down in the chair next to him.

The two Montgomery men took their seats.

"Now, I asked you two here because I've counseled you and declared you both ready for marriage but I need to know if that's still the case. Right now there are people at the church, they've been working all night well into this morning transforming the sanctuary for today's wedding. The setup they've done is incredible but I will shut it all down if I don't hear what I need to from the both of you this morning." Bishop announced.

Not expecting to hear those words, Carson cocked his head to the side and said, "You'd cancel the wedding?"

Unwavering in his decision, Bishop quickly replied, "Oh most definitely. Carson, even with you being my son, there's no way, I'd allow, under my watch for you to marry Scarlett or anybody for that fact if you didn't mean them any good."

Shocked by Bishop's words, Scarlett shifted her weight in her seat but she was unable to feel the heaviness of them because of her inability to focus. She was drifting in and out of thoughts from the night before.

Although Bishop's eyes were heavy from carrying around his missed sleep, he kept a steady watch on Carson and Scarlett. He carefully watched and read their body language, he wanted to observe what they said up against what they weren't saying either.

Folding his hands on top of his desk, Bishop replied, "Now, as your spiritual counsel and spiritual covering, I need to hear from the two of you as to your intentions. Do you still want to get married? Carson, I want to hear from you first and then Scarlett, I want to hear from you, is that alright with you sweetheart?"

Bishop took a stern approach with Carson but seeing Scarlett as a victim of his son's immature ignorance, he coddled her.

"In fact, let's do this...Carson, I want you to leave the room so Scarlett and I can talk privately. Now go outside." Bishop Montgomery said dismissing Carson.

Scarlett dropped her chin to her chest and pressed her hands against her cheeks. Sitting alone under the watchful scrutiny of Bishop caused her to tremble somewhat on the inside.

"Oh Lord, why is he singling me out and is it just me or is he being overly nice to me?" Scarlett thought."

"You doing alright this morning Scarlett?"

"Yes sir, I am."

The strain in the conversation was rigid.

Carson paced the halls wringing his hands as he tried to eavesdrop through the walls to see if he could hear any part of their conversation.

"You say you're doing alright but I just have one simple question for you, do you still want to marry my son?" Bishop inquired.

Taking a long pause before answering, Scarlett scratched her cheek and said, "To be honest with you Bishop, I don't know anymore."

"Okay, I can understand that but let me ask you this? Do you still love him?" Bishop asked.

"Well of course, a person can't just turn off their feelings overnight." Scarlett said aloud while thinking inside, "*Or can they?*" As she thought about her reunion with Gregory.

"On the one hand, when I got here almost a week ago, I was thrilled to be here; I couldn't wait for this week to end so I could be married to Carson. But now, with everything that's happened, it's hard to process how I feel because trust me, I know people make mistakes and can get caught up in things they weren't planning. I can't think of anyone who gets up in the morning with intentions on hurting the people they love and care for. Can you?" Scarlett shared.

"Not at all and I can tell by what you just said that you have compassion towards Carson and what has happened. I tell you what though, I will not marry you two if I'm not certain you all want this. From what I hearing from you, I'm leaning towards not. I would rather preside over your funeral than this wedding." Bishop revealed.

Knocking on the door, Carson peered his head through the door, "I'm sorry to interrupt but may I come in, I have something I'd like to say, if I could."

Replying in a sharp tone, Bishop said, "Come on in Carson. What do you have to say for yourself?"

Walking directly towards Scarlett, Carson stopped in front of her and fell to one knee.

"From the first day you walked into our church; I knew it wouldn't be your last time. I could feel you and I would be connected for ever. Scarlett, I'm not perfect, I've never claimed to be but what is perfect is love. The bible says it casts out all fear[4]. I know you're scared and afraid and I can't blame you for that but I need you to know I love you with all of my heart and I'm ready to be the man you need and deserve. I'm so sorry for hurting you and I pray you can forgive me. I'm ready to be the man God has called me to be." Carson fumbled around in his pocket and pulled out a smooth, glossy box. "I was going to do this and present you with a larger ring at the wedding but I want to do this now because I want to propose to you...again. I promise Scarlett baby that I'm in this thing if you'll have me. I love you and I'd love to prove it to you if you will do me the honors by becoming my wife today. Scarlett, will you marry me?" Carson said with tears and wet eyes.

---

[4] **1 John 4:18**: "There is no fear in love. But perfect love drives out fear, because fear has to do with punishment. The one who fears is not made perfect in love." (**NIV**)

Chapter 35

"Sooo, spill the beans honey; I need to know from top to bottom everything that happened. What did Bishop Montgomery want with you? Come on girl, you're taking too long, is there going to be a wedding today or not?" Sherry asked.

Taking notice and drooling over the brilliantly shining ring on Scarlett's lifted hand, Kelly gawked saying, "Based on this new bling on her finger, I'm guessing that's a yes."

A faint knock on the door interrupted the girl talk.

"Come in." They all said laughing and giggling.

At Minta's entrance, a quieted hush fell over the room.

"Good morning ladies, don't stop all of the laughter and fun just because I walked in." Minta said.

Each of the ladies in the room looked around the room trying to find a source of comfort as the moment was quite uncomfortable.

Picking up on the slight chill from the women in the room, Minta asked warmly, "Would you ladies mind if I had a few minutes with my daughter?"

Everyone in the room slowly cleared out and left Minta and Scarlett behind.

Sitting down on the bed across from Scarlett, Minta said, "Good morning, if you care to see, I brought you something." Minta said. "I haven't seen or talked with you much since the other day but I wanted to come by and talk with you this morning if that's alright."

Pulling at her ear, Scarlett asked, "So what'd you bring?"

Opening a beautifully wrapped in fabric and lace photo album, Minta said smiling, "This is a photo album of you from birth to your college graduation. A book of memories of my baby."

Seeing pictures from her past, some she'd never even seen before, some with her favorite doll, Marilene, she felt assured about her future. She smiled and then the smiles turned into tears and full on crying.

Minta removed the album from between the two of them and sat next to Scarlett to embrace her, "I'm so sorry sweetheart and I'm asking for your forgiveness; I never meant to hurt you." Minta said rocking back and forth with Scarlett in her arms. "I thought I was doing the best thing for you but it's not worth me losing you in the process. So, whatever you decide to do sweetheart; I'm here for you."

In a tone that lacked enthusiasm, Scarlett replied, "When you look at these pictures, you see a happy baby that grew up to become a happy woman.

To me, that means that you did your job as a mother. You've raised me to be the woman I am today and I'm grateful for that. Not that I won't need you anymore but it's time for you to let me keep growing, on my own."

Wiping tears away from both Scarlett's face and her own, Minta said, "I can respect that and even if I can't, I'm going to have to. I love you Scarlett."

"I love you too mama." Scarlett replied.

Chapter 36

"Hey everybody, let's gather around, I think they are about to leave." Regina announced.

At the Montgomery estate, the core family and friends were hanging out and winding down from the day's event.

Carson and Scarlett were married and about to leave for their honeymoon.

"Before the newlyweds leave, I'd like to cover them in prayer. This has been some kind of week, huh? We've yelled, we've cried, we've endured much but we're here. We've had some highs and some lows but we made it." In a sermon-like voice, Bishop continued, "All I can say is, thanks be to God who causes us to triumph."

Regina broke out into a popular worship song and George followed behind her singing, *"Thanks be to God who always causes us to triumph in His name. Thanks be to God who always causes us to win, yeah. Thanks be to God who always causes us to triumph in His name. Thanks be to God. Thanks be to God."*

"You see family, this is what it's all about...no matter what comes our way, through the power of Jesus Christ, He makes the way for us to triumph and have victory. For all this couple and this family have been through this week, I want to say, we are victorious and triumphant. As you two prepare to leave, it is my prayer that you two will have a blessed life, one filled with happiness."

Stepping in and taking over where Bishop ended, Regina said, "I agree with my husband and if I could add one thing, Scarlett, we love you and we're so happy to have you be a part of our family. Now go on to your honeymoon and make me some grandbabies; I'm ready to be called Grandma Regina. Remember honey, the fruit of your womb is blessed and whoever the Lord blesses you two with will be blessed."

George stepped up and addressed the couple, "Scarlett, baby I'm so proud of you, you were a beautiful bride and it was my absolute pleasure to walk you down the aisle today." Turning his attentions towards his new son-in-law, George said, "Carson, I hope you remember our talk, take care of my daughter because if you don't, you better have the fire department's number on speed dial."

Reaching in for a hug, Carson replied, "I promise sir; I'll be sure to take excellent care of her."

Minta took her turn to speak with the couple, "My beautiful daughter, you were a vision of perfection today, a beautiful bride, just like I always knew you would be. I'd like to apologize again to the two of you and I wish nothing but the best for you. I love you Scarlett...and you too, Carson."

Scarlett, Carson, and Minta share in a reconciliatory embrace.

Making their way down the line, Mother Montgomery hugged the couple and said, "So you're married now, just like this past week, as you go through life, you'll have many ups and downs, I just pray your up and down will be more in your bedroom."

Red faces flushed across everyone in the room as they laughed at Mother's witty commentary.

Sherry and Glenn rounded out the line, bringing up the rear.

"Congratulations you two." Sherry said.

"Thank you guys, so, I guess we'll see you two next month, when you two tie the knot, huh?" Carson said.

Smiling at each other, Glenn kissed Sherry and announced, "No, not at all. We got married this afternoon after you two did."

Sherry flashed her makeshift wedding ring in front of everyone as she beamed with pride. "I's married now, I say I's married now y'all."

"Sherry approached me and asked for Minta and I to stand for them and with them in between the wedding and the reception today and Minta married them this afternoon. Both of my girls got married today." George pronounced.

"Beautiful, this is just beautiful." Regina echoed.

Everyone continued to share hugs, kisses, and well-wishes to now both Carson, Scarlett, Sherry and Glenn.

"This is what family is all about." Bishop exclaimed.

Holding Scarlett's hand in his, Carson said, "Well, this is all lovely and all but before the sun sets, me and my WIFE must get going. The "mile high" club awaits us, sunsets are breathtaking from the jet."

Covering her face with her hands, Scarlett shook her head saying, "Carson...you are too much. I can already see life with you will bring forth many surprises."

Waving at her daughter, Minta thought to herself, *"She has no idea."*

Epilogue

"In all my years, I don't' think we've ever had a wedding week quite like this one ever before at Wondrous Works Tabernacle Fellowship, this has truly been one heck of week, wouldn't you say?"

"Regina and I are hopeful and prayerful that Carson will begin to confirm his calling and election sure, for if he does these things, according to the scriptures, he won't at any time ever stumble again."

"I came real close to calling off the entire ceremony, I'd made up my mind but my son showed me a side of him that I'd been wanting to see for a long time. He acknowledged his wrongs and took responsibility for his actions."

"Now, only God knows what the future holds but I choose to put my faith and trust in Him that no matter what happens, He's Lord over all of it."

"Listen to me my dear brothers and sisters, this life doesn't come without times of testing, trials and tribulations, I read somewhere the best of men would faint, if they did not receive mercy from God. That mercy is here to help us out and on throughout to life's end."

"No, my son's not perfect but I'm praying for him and I hope you are too. Regina accused me of glorifying sin in our children, do you agree with her? I certainly don't want to do that. My prayer is that one day, Carson submits himself under the mighty hand of God so that our Heavenly Father may be glorified through his life. However, until then, I ask you to join me with praying for Carson and Scarlett. I ask you to join me in praying for all of our family. We who are strong ought to bear with the failings of the weak and not to please ourselves. Pray for the Montgomery and Watson family and we'll be sure and pray for you and yours."

"If you'll agree to join me in prayer, have any ideas, recommendations, or advice on how I can effectively ensure Carson's ready for this mantle, email me at shakirabelieves@gmail.com with the subject line, "Advice for Bishop," and help me out. I'd love to hear from each of you."

"Now, may the Lord bless you and keep you. May the Lord make His face to shine upon you and be gracious to you; may the Lord lift up His countenance upon you and give you peace. In Jesus' name. Amen."

~Bishop Montgomery

Psalm 119:147

"I rise early, before the sun is up; I cry out for help and put my hope in your words." (NIV)

ABOUT THE AUTHOR

Shakira R. Thompson, a natural born storyteller who submitted to her God-given talents and in doing so, God showed up and made her a **BELIEVER.** He's transformed her into an author, publisher, and entrepreneur.

She is the founder of **Believer's Choice Media,** an inspirational content company dedicated to encouraging believers to live the life they were created to live on earth and beyond.   She's penned five, well-received inspirational fiction novels with a sixth on the way.

With a renewed sense of purpose, Shakira is not only writing and speaking, she's living...living her life according to Ephesians 2:10:

"For we are his workmanship, created in Christ Jesus unto good works, which God hath before ordained that we should walk in them." (KJV)

Shakira is a proud Alumni of Florida A&M University in Tallahassee, Florida where she holds a B.S in Business Administration as well as an M.B.A. with a concentration in Supply Chain Management.

Shakira has always delved in the world of real estate, but most recently made it official. She is a

Realtor®, licensed in the State of Florida, where she's the listing agent for EquityPro. Naturally, she's expanding the Believer's Choice brand and is in the process of developing Believer's Choice Realty, LLC.

Living her life with purpose has pushed her into her latest venture, co-hosting *The Dee Lee Show,* where she has the opportunity to encourage **BELIEVERS** over the airwaves.

Although Shakira may wear many hats these days, the most important role to her, is that of wife and mother.

Born and raised in Fernandina Beach, Florida, she now resides in Orlando, Florida with her family.

A SNEAK PEEK

Glow In The Dark

"Yep, I'll take that, this seat has my name written all over it, I guess I've done something right in my life."

Thinking to herself, Chelsea Douglas rushed over to claim a newly empty table in the trendy and quite popular coffee bar, *CiCo*, meaning coffee in, coffee out.

While it was filled with people, enjoying their contemporary single origin coffee drinks and organic, fair traded teas, the vibe and atmosphere provided a work space of creativity and serenity, unlike the tiny apartment Chelsea called home.

Sipping her favorite drink, a vanilla bean latte sourced directly from Central America, Chelsea carefully sat up her laptop and headphones and went to work, well at least she hoped to work. She scourged the Internet looking for work.

Funding for the arts and musical programs at Chelsea's former school were the first to be rerouted to other programs and Chelsea's job as the beloved music teacher was rerouted as well...out of the door.

With the summer half over, Chelsea's job became finding one.

Deep into her searching, Chelsea was slightly distracted as she returned a nod and smile at a young woman sitting in front of her. The young woman got up and walked past Chelsea towards the direction of the restrooms.

Minutes later, she returned. Glancing back at Chelsea again, she smiled one more time but the smile was filled with unease.

Rocking in her seat, Mariah could feel her heart beating faster, she spoke a few words under her breath, took another sip of her drink and got up from her seat once again.

Trying to steady her shaking mug, Mariah stood at Chelsea's table and said, "Um excuse me, do you mind if I sit down and talk with you for a minute?"

"What?!" Chelsea responded. Removing her headphones, she asked, "I'm sorry, what did you say?"

Stumbling over her words, Mariah said, "Oh no, you're fine, I was just wondering if you would mind if I sat here and talked with you for a moment."

Shrugging her shoulders, Chelsea replied, "Sure, have a seat, what's up?"

Taking a quick breath, Mariah said, "I hope you don't get too weirded out but I've been struggling with whether or not I should say something to you. I'm very nervous but I have to be obedient and tell you what He wants me to say."

"He who? Who in here wants you to tell me something? Aren't we a little too old for that, are you someone's wing man or something like that? Listen, for one, I don't have time for a man and two, I especially don't have time for one who can't talk to me straight up." Chelsea said laughing.

Mariah's quick, high-pitched laughter instantly made Chelsea and herself for that matter, uncomfortable.

Shaking out her hands, Mariah calmed down and said, "No, no, no, it's nothing like that. This is a message from God."

Chelsea's downturned mouth slipped into sarcasm mode, a common defense mechanism for her, "Oh I think I'd rather hear from the guy who's too scared to talk to me."

Mariah's emotion-choked voice said, "Hey, this isn't a joke."

Chelsea quickly replied, "Sounds like one to me."

"I noticed you when you walked in and I heard the voice of the Lord speak to me about you. I shrugged it off. Then when you sat down, I heard Him speak again, this time it was a little louder. I then began talking to Him, asking Him why did He want me to go up to a complete stranger and say what He was telling me. You see, I talk to Him like that. His voice kept getting stronger and louder until I couldn't take it anymore so I got up and walked to the restroom to pray and gather my nerves. I've been praying about Him using me more but I had no idea that today would be a day of testing for me. So, here I am, sitting here at your table with something to tell you, if you'd like to hear it, Chelsea." Mariah explained.

Struck with an unexpected feeling of both wonder and fear, Chelsea said, "Hey wait, how do you know my name?"

"I know a little more than that if you'd let me share." Mariah said.

Slapping her knee and laughing out loud, Chelsea pointed at Mariah and said, "You almost had me, God didn't tell you my name; you heard it when they called me up for my drink order. Girl, you had me going for a second but this is all crazy because don't you know Christianity is a made up religion, it's baseless. I read last week that a bible scholar no doubt came out and said that the story of Jesus Christ is all a Roman hoax and was made up to control the minds of people. You haven't heard about that?"

Clearing her throat, Mariah answered by saying, "No, I hadn't heard about that but whether it's true or not, I like what Albert Camus once said, "I would rather live my life as if there is a God and die to find out there isn't, than to live as if there isn't and to die to find out that there is."

Taking a long pause before responding, Chelsea drank from her cup and then said, "Hmph, that's deep girl, real deep."

Grabbing her cup, Mariah said, "You may not be taking this seriously but I do. Yeah, I was nervous at first but righteous indignation has arisen in me and must say what thus saith the Lord, whether you want to hear it or not. I will not let you stand in the way of me doing what the Lord has asked of me."

Rolling her eyes, Chelsea sat back in her seat with her hands folded and said, "Alright then, lay it on me, what's this all important message from the Almighty God who speaks to you but not to me."

Placing her hand on her chest, Mariah began by saying, "For the record, I heard your name when you walked through the door, hearing it at the counter only confirmed to me what the Lord was already saying." Testing the waters a bit, Mariah eased in by asking, "Does the scripture, Jeremiah 29:11[5] mean anything to you?"

Chelsea's expression blanched pale as her wet eyes widened. In her heart, she said, *My mother used to say that scripture over me every night from the day she found out she was pregnant with me.*

Mariah could see a softening with Chelsea and continued, "I heard Him say, He has need of you. He says, yes, you're going through a dark time now, a difficult time but that He sees all and knows all. He told me to tell you, He's been with you since the time in your mother's womb. He says, He's going to use you to be a light in a darkened world, that where you don't see a way out, He's already made one for you. The life you seek is already seeking you. He says, you are seeking after a career but He's inviting you to accept the calling He's placed on your life. He says if you'll trust Him and learn to enter into His rest, you'll never work another day in your life because what He

---

[5] Jeremiah 29:11: "For I know the plans I have for you," declares the LORD, "plans to prosper you and not to harm you, plans to give you hope and a future."

has for you will never again feel like work but purpose and destiny."

Rising from the table, without saying anything, Mariah walked away to grab some napkins.

Wiping her eyes, Chelsea spoke out, "Hey, where are you going? You can't just say things like that and walk away."

Plopping a stack of napkins on the table, Mariah smiled and said, "I was trying to be nice and grab you some napkins."

The two ladies shared a laugh.

"Well, thank you...I guess." Chelsea said.

Extending her hand, Mariah said, "I know I started out a little shaky so I didn't ever get a chance to introduce myself but my name is Mariah. I promise I'm not going to take up anymore of your time but I hope you know; I had to do that and I pray it meant something to you. Be blessed."

Looking around the crowded coffee bar, Chelsea realized Mariah's seat had been taken and said, "No, please sit down, I'd like to continue talking to you...if you don't mind...and I'm Chelsea by the way."

Mariah smiled and said, "Okay Chelsea, it's nice to officially meet you and no, I don't mind. Uh, before I sit down, would you like another vanilla bean latte? That is what you're drinking right?"

The high-priced drinks menu at *CiCo* flashed across Chelsea's mind, *CiCo* wasn't in her limited budget and the gift cards she received from students at the end of the school year were starting to dwindle.

Heading away from the table, Mariah added, "Hey listen, it's on me, I just wondered if you wanted the same thing or if you wanted to try something else."

Smiling, Chelsea played along and said, "Oh yeah, yeah, I was just looking at the menu to see if I wanted to try something different, but you know what, the vanilla latte is fine, thanks."

NOTE FROM THE AUTHOR
Final Thoughts

With each and every book I'm blessed to write, I'm oftentimes humbled as well as honored to be able to do so.

Nothing about this journey is easy but let me tell you, as I keep going, I'm finding, it's so worth it.

Being afforded the opportunity to write what some call realistic fiction, offers me the opportunity to witness first hand and show others through these words that redemption is available to all, no matter how flawed. It is important to note, God will use ALL people for the good of HIS will.

When we're willing to expose our flaws, we can receive the flawlessness of Christ. Our flaws illustrate to us on a daily basis that God is still in the miracle working business.

Think about it, God has unlimited power, He could choose whomever and whatever He desired to perform His will, things more excellent than you and I. BUT, God in His grace and mercy chooses to work through the frailties of mankind.

The design of the enemy is to keep us in darkness to extinguish the light of Christ that we want so dearly in our hearts. Christ wants us to be a light in the world and to shine consistently.

The problem is we think once we've accepted Christ, we're done and so we many times find ourselves in unfavorable and unflattering situations. Until we, including myself, and the characters in these books realize that, I'll always have content to write about. These characters help me to understand how I shouldn't take myself so seriously and to allow God to have His way in my life.

In *Unforsaken*, I said in my final thoughts that it was going to be the last in the series...boy was I wrong!

I've now to come to realize that these stories don't just belong to me but to others and as life would have it, another book was birthed.

If you're familiar with me at all, you know already the story I tell of how I was in the midst of writing The Love Bug and High Noon Justice hijacked its spot and took over. Well, wouldn't you know, the same, exact thing happened with this book. I was in the process of writing, *Glow In the Dark*, (you've just read it's preview and I hope you'll be on the lookout for it) when *Before The Sun*, decided it wanted to go first. Six books in, I let the characters tell me where they want to go and I follow. You've just read the result of the latest hijacking.

While *Before the Sun* doesn't follow the prescription of scripture found in Psalms 37, it is where we learn how everything started to bring us to *High Noon Justice*, then to *The Big Bonanza*, to lastly *Unforsaken*.

ONE LAST THING...

As always, I pray you've enjoyed the prequel to the Psalms 37 series. If you believe your family and friends would love it too, please feel free to spread the word and tell them about it.

In addition, beyond talking about it, I'd love if you'd write about it as well. Posting an online review wherever you hang out online, whether it's on Amazon, Goodreads, social media, you name it, shares your experience with these books. I'm on all of them and I'd love to hear your thoughts and feedback.

For more information about what's going on with me, for latest news and announcements, book updates, simply ready to believe and so much more, please head over to www.shakirabelieves.com and sign up.

Not if but when you're facing any type of trial, remember the word of God says, Weeping may endure for a night but joy comes in the morning. As believers, we have a blessed assurance that we can rise **Before the Sun** and cry for help and we can confidently put our hope in His word that He'll be careful to perform.

All the best,

~ Shakira

OTHER BELIEVERS CHOICE MEDIA STORIES YOU MAY ENJOY

High Noon Justice

http://amzn.com/B00NDE3WAK

The Big Bonanza

http://amzn.com/B00RKV1VEG

Unforsaken

http://amzn.com/B019NNFIQA

The Love Bug

http://amzn.com/B00PSXAWV6

Candy Coated Christmas

http://amzn.com/B00QCEJMKW

www.ingramcontent.com/pod-product-compliance
Lightning Source LLC
Chambersburg PA
CBHW051246250626
47155CB00009B/3185